MURDER WITH MONEY

BLYTHE BAKER

When Sylvia's sister disappears unexpectedly, Sylvia doubts the official story. Joan wouldn't run off to California to become a film star without first saying goodbye to her family. Clearly, she's in some sort of danger and it's up to Sylvia to find out what.

But can Sylvia set aside her doubts about her mysterious butler in order to enlist help from Miles when she needs it most?

1

As I walked away from the letter lying open on my bed, I asked myself why I was so unnerved by its contents. I had confronted murderers before. What was so different about Miles?

I trusted him...that is why it's so different.

I went over to the window and gazed out. How different my life became the night that my uncle died. I never would have met Miles...but never would have gotten caught up in all these investigations either. Was that what I wished?

At this point, I didn't know.

I had to speak with him. I could not delay any longer.

How was I going to go about it? What was I going to say?

I shook my head. That sort of thing didn't matter. If I asked to speak with him, I knew he would agree.

I steeled myself. Now was as good a time as any, was it not?

I picked up the letter from the bed, folded it, and tucked it into my pocket.

I left my room, resolute and determined.

I found him down in the parlor, preparing it for our family's after dinner time.

He straightened when I came in. "Miss Sylvia," he said, smiling at me. "Can I help you?"

"Miles, I need to speak with you."

With that, I closed the double doors behind me, closing myself in with him.

I never much liked the parlor at the back of the house. It may very well have overlooked the river, and enjoyed some of the best and brightest light first thing in the morning, but it always felt dank and cold.

Even now as I slid home the lock on the pair of double doors, I had to suppress a shiver.

The fireplace along the wall opposite to the windows sat dark, the morning's fire long since gone out without anyone residing within to require its stoking. It seemed that the only regular visitors to this room were me and Joan, and occasionally Mother after dinner if she had company. It might have been due to the low ceilings or even the lack of comfortable furniture...but perhaps more than anything, as of late, it held too many reminders.

The night Uncle Walter fell from the balcony ten stories above at the grand opening of The Vandegrift Hotel, my family had briefly gathered in this room together with a great hush of utter disbelief. Mrs. Riley had brought us food and drink, neither of which was consumed. This small, dark room was not a haven then, as much as it had felt like stark, cold torment.

I released a small, pent up sigh from between my lips, and turned to face the reason I had come into this room now, pleased to find it almost empty.

Empty all except for Miles.

He stood near the hearth, brushing soot from his arms; the logs beside the fireplace had been replenished for the evening. His brow had furrowed, the wrinkles on his forehead in deep relief in the dim lighting of the solitary lit lamp on the writing hutch.

Those green eyes of his fixed on me, and it astounded me just how quickly I had forgotten the strength of them during my time away in Newport. "You look quite troubled," he said, his tone marred with worry. "What has happened?"

I did not know where to begin. I supposed the beginning was always the best, but I knew that I must tread carefully.

I drew my hands behind my back, grazing the inside of my left wrist with the forefinger of my right hand. *Yes, it's still there,* I assured myself, feeling a letter opener I had tucked inside my sleeve just before leaving my room. A poor excuse for a weapon, but it might be able to buy me some time if he attacked me. And I had his pistol, locked securely away in my lockbox in my room. I had checked to make sure it was still there just before coming down.

I cleared my throat. "There is...something that I must discuss with you," I said. "Something that I have been meaning to discuss with you for some time, but never had the courage."

He stiffened, adjusting his footing. "What is it?" he asked. He did not sound particularly worried, but even from where I stood across the room, I could see the strain around his eyes.

"You have been working here, serving my family since the end of October," I began. "That is nearly three full months now that you have been beneath our roof, aiding my father and mother, taking care of our needs to the best of your ability. I should like to begin by commending you for your exemplary work. You seem to have more experience and talent than I had expected."

He nodded his thanks. "Well, I am most grateful to hear you say so," he said. "I am honored by such praise. Truly."

"However," I went on, "there is still something that eludes me, as well as the rest of my family." *There is little reason to make this seem as if I am coming at him entirely on my own.* "We know very little about you. We know your character, at least what you allow us to see, but apart from that, we know nothing. Your past is entirely a mystery to us, and if I am honest, that is somewhat unsettling."

Miles' face shadowed, and he looked away. "My past is of little importance," he said. "I can assure you of that."

"Are you certain?" I asked. "Or is there something in your past that you want to hide?"

He looked at me and met my gaze with far more ease than I might have expected. "What could I possibly have to hide?"

I steeled myself, balling my hands into fists. There was no turning back now. "A murdered wife, for one thing."

The chill I had anticipated flooded the room like a mist before a terrible storm. It seemed to sap the very life out of the air, along with any warmth or sound.

How could he deny it when I so starkly told him exactly what it was that he was hiding? If it wasn't true, then he would question what in the world I was talking about. Then again, he might try to do that even if he was guilty. I did not expect him to admit to it, not at the outset. I had dealt with enough true murderers at this point to know that they often had to feel there was little to no means of escape before they admitted to their crimes. With Miles, though, it was difficult to know what he might do.

I certainly wish I could predict his actions... I thought. Typically, I believed that I would be able to do so. But as worried as I was, I didn't even know if I would be able to find my way out of an argument without falling over myself...

And so I waited. I watched, and waited.

He moved little. His eyes continued to bore into the back of the armchair nearest him, an ugly thing with green paisley upholstery. If I did not know any better, I would have thought him frozen in place.

"What do you know?"

It struck me like a sack full of bricks. I had expected him to become angry, to deny it, maybe even to laugh at me. But he did nothing of the sort. His tone remained neutral, and the question really did not confirm or deny anything.

"I know everything – " I started to say.

"No," he said, a bit more firmly. "I am quite certain you do not, or you wouldn't have said it as you did. Now, I shall only ask you one more time, Miss Sylvia. What, precisely, do you know?"

I hesitated at his tone, but supposed I owed him a fair chance to explain himself.

"Very well," I said. "I shall start at the beginning."

"That would be for the best, I think," he said.

"When you were hired, we had to move your things

to the room in which you currently reside, out of the room you were first placed in," I said. "Do you remember? I helped to move some of your items, including a few of your books. At one point, I nearly tripped, several of the books falling out of my hands..." I paused. I had rehearsed this time and again in my head for the past few weeks. "A newspaper clipping slipped out from the front cover of one book, and I caught a glimpse of it. Perhaps I had no right to read it...but it is what started me down this path in the first place."

Miles ducked his head. "You read through my personal belongings?" he asked.

"You must understand why it caught my attention," I said. "We had just lost my uncle, the murder which you helped me to solve. Upon seeing the news article, I feared that you had also experienced some sort of tragic loss just as we had. I thought it might explain the very reason why you did not wish to discuss your past. However..." I looked straight at him, my heart sinking. "I saw the photograph of the woman found dead in Hyde Park, and the man beside her...who looked exactly like you."

Miles stared at me, his jaw working. "I will give you that. The photograph is indeed of me...and my late wife."

My eyes widened. "So it's true – "

"Is that all you are basing assumptions on?" Miles

asked. "I highly doubt that, knowing what an astute detective you've become. Why don't you finish sharing your story before you start with the inevitable accusations?"

I sniffed, but he was right. There was still a great deal more. "Very well," I said. "After I found the article, I decided that I must have misunderstood something. I thought that it was entirely possible I was missing information. However, then I caught you throwing something away in the river, under the cover of darkness, clearly hoping that you would not be seen by anyone. It heightened my suspicions once again."

Miles' face hardened. "You followed me?"

"You were behaving suspiciously," I said. "And if you had murdered your own wife, as the article suggested, then why would I allow that to slide? You could be a threat to me and my family."

Miles frowned, and said nothing.

"I happened upon a fisherman whose boat I recognized, and managed to flag him down. I asked him to seek out the parcel you had thrown away, knowing how futile it likely was. However, it wasn't terribly long before he showed up at our house with the package in hand...and I discovered a firearm."

Now it seemed that he couldn't look at me. "You have been thorough, haven't you?" he asked.

"Even so, I knew that I was only discovering pieces of

the story, and as such, I decided to pen one of my friends in London. I asked her if she had heard anything about the death of a woman that had been found in Hyde Park. Once again, I knew that it might be a sliver of a chance..." I sighed, shaking my head. "It seems that the truth always comes to the surface, though, doesn't it? I received a letter from said friend while I was visiting my family in Newport, and have only just read it a short while ago..."

I pulled the letter from my pocket, and showed it to him.

"The description of the murder is what surprised me the most. Apparently, a man she had been walking with in the park looked a great deal like you. It seems that while they were walking together, he pulled out a gun, a gun that was never found by the authorities, and shot her right in the middle of – "

"Stop!" Miles said with a snap. "Please. I do not need to hear any more."

He didn't want to relive that night, it seemed. Was it guilt? Was it too much to bear? "But I am not yet finished," I said. "There is more to the letter, wherein my friend told me that the man who had attacked the victim so brazenly had yet to be found. Which means that if it did happen to be you, then it could explain how both you and the gun were missing...and now hiding here, in my family's house."

Miles began to shake his head, still unable to meet

my gaze. "Sylvia, you know so little of what you speak..."

I glared at him. How dare he think he could use my name in such a familiar manner?

"You have yet to deny these claims," I said. "Which makes me think you have little reason to deny them. And if that is the case, then what is preventing me from going straight to the police and telling them what I have learned?"

"I suppose you wouldn't know, but I have made it a point to make friends with the local police department," Miles said. "One highly placed officer in particular. I have earned his trust."

"By lying to him?" I asked, my voice rising.

"Of course not," he said. "I knew there might come a time where I needed the help of the police, and was simply preparing myself. Is that not wisdom?"

"If you were preparing to get them on your side so that you could hide from the London authorities, then I suppose it is wisdom to save your own hide," I chided.

"I am astonished you would believe this without question," Miles said.

"What would you have me do, ignore the facts that have piled up against you?" I asked.

"Facts that do seem rather convenient, don't they?" he asked.

"How so?" I asked.

"You have seen enough cases, experienced enough

of these malicious acts to know when someone is capable of such crimes, yes?" he asked. "Think for a moment. Really think about it. Do you truly believe I would have done this?"

"How can you ask me that?" I asked. "I hardly know you – "

"Yet you have trusted me to watch your back, to save your life on more than one occasion. If you really thought I had killed my own wife, would you have trusted me for a second beside you, chasing real murderers around?"

It annoyed me how accurate he was with his words, how correct about how I felt. That was the same question I had asked myself over and over again, wasn't it? Why had I trusted him?

"I want you to look at me and tell me that you honestly believe I could have killed my wife," Miles said. "Tell me."

I hesitated. This conversation was meant to be from me to him, not the other way around. How did it turn against me? He had no right to be the one who was angry.

I could only stare at him for a moment. After all this time, all I had wanted to do was ask him about this, to confront him, for him to give me the facts.

Now, I didn't know what to do. I didn't even know what to say.

"I will tell you the truth, the whole of it," he began,

breathing heavily, his forehead wrinkled with concern. "But first, I would appreciate hearing that you do not believe me guilty."

"That is your caveat?" I asked. "That I must admit it before you will tell the truth? Why not try to convince me?"

"Because – "

The door handles behind me began to shake, quickly followed by a sharp, shrill banging. "Sylvie? Joanie? Are you in here?"

My heart thundered in my chest, and I shot one more glare at Miles. It seemed that the rest of our conversation would have to wait. "Mother, it is only Miles and I," I said, hurrying to unlock the doors.

When I pulled them open, I froze at the sight of her stricken face. "What's the matter?" I asked.

"Have you seen your sister?" she asked.

2

_____

My brow furrowed. "Of course," I said. "She and I were in the drawing room together a little over an hour ago. Why?"

"She isn't there now," Mother said, wringing her hands together. She peered past me into the parlor as Miles approached.

"Is everything all right?" he asked.

"We cannot find Joan," Mother said. "She isn't in her room, and she is not in the parlor. Are you sure she isn't in here with you?"

"No, Mother, you can see for yourself that she isn't," I said.

Mother's face fell. "You do not suppose..."

"What?" I asked.

"Let's not panic quite yet, Mrs. Shipman," Miles said. "Have you checked the back garden? While Miss

Sylvia was gone, Miss Joan enjoyed spending time out there, at least for brief periods."

"Sylvia…" Mother said, her expression quite grim. "She kept talking about these…these terrible ideas while you were gone. She was so jealous that you had the chance to leave, kept regretting the fact that she had not gone with you… She kept saying how all she wanted to do was get away – "

"Allow me to go round up some of the servants and we shall search," Miles said, sweeping past us and down the hall.

"The last time you saw her was an hour ago?" Mother repeated. "What were you two doing?"

"Having our afternoon coffee," I said. "We were simply talking about my trip to see Michael, and the goings on here while I was away."

"Did she say anything strange? Anything to indicate where she might have gone?" she asked.

"No, of course not," I said, the small hairs at the back of my neck standing up.

"And where did you go after that?"

My face flushed slightly. "I went to my room to read a letter that had arrived for me while I was out of town," I said. "And then I came down here to the parlor to – to check something with Miles."

"And you did not see Joan at all during that time?" she asked.

"Mother, how have you gotten it into your head

that she might have – might have run away or some such nonsense?"

"I know my own children," Mother said, her face tightening. "Lately, I have heard a sorrow in her voice that I have never heard before. I thought it was simply because she missed you, but now I think there was something more to it."

A sickening pit formed in my stomach, and I tried to squash it before it became any stronger. I knew what she was talking about. I had thought Joan had been speaking a bit wistfully recently, too, but there were seasons where she became like that in the past. I always attributed it to her artistic nature, with all her love of the theater, but those moods would pass with time. If all she wanted was to travel, then that would have been easy enough to fix with some strategic planning.

"Well, if what she wanted was a change of scene, I know that money might be a little tighter than usual, but she might be able to go and visit Michael and Penelope just as I did," I said. "I am certain they would be happy to have her for a few weeks. She might have to wait until – "

"Sylvia, I think she really is gone..." Mother interrupted, and then she dissolved into tears, grabbing hold of me and burying her face into my shoulder.

All I could do was stand there and gape at the top of her head. I had heard my mother cry on many occasions, but it was typically after she had been with her friends and perhaps indulged a bit too much in food and drink. And it was never about anything important.

She was truly afraid, and what surprised me was how only an hour had passed and she had already so utterly convinced herself that something had happened. Joan might have gone any number of places, even at this hour. Out for a walk, or to call on a friend. Maybe she simply forgot to tell anyone she was leaving the house. She was not a child, after all, and could come and go as she pleased.

And yet, perhaps there was such a thing as a mother's intuition. I could not entirely dismiss Mother's fears.

"Have you spoken to Father?" I asked.

"Not yet," Mother said, sniffling. "I did not wish to worry him."

The sound of footsteps on the stairs drew my eyes upward, and predictably we heard the noise of doors opening and closing.

Looking for Joan, I thought. *She is going to feel so foolish when they find her and when she learns that she worried Mother for absolutely no reason.*

My heart quickened as they continued to search the rooms overhead. Ten minutes passed, and another pair of servants came running down the stairs to feverishly check the other rooms on the lower floor.

This could be bad, I admitted to myself. *They still cannot find her.*

The worst thing I could do right now was allow my Mother's wild imagination to take hold of my own thoughts. I could not allow my fears to run away with me, lest I lose the logical thinking that could prove useful at such a time.

Miles reappeared at the bottom of the staircase, turning around to come and stand with us.

"I am sorry to say that she has not yet been found in any of her usual places," Miles said. I could see the worry creasing his forehead again. *Was that because of our conversation? Or because of Joan?* Maybe it was both.

"Oh, dear..." Mother said, laying her hands on either side of her face, her eyes blank. "Oh, heavens. This cannot be happening. Where could she be?"

"I would remain calm, madam," Miles said. "We are still searching. Perhaps she has visited the kitchens for something to eat, or perhaps she has fallen asleep in Mr. Shipman's study. There are still many explanations for where she could have gone without anyone's knowledge – "

"She is gone far away. I just know she is..." Mother said with a shaky sob.

I looked at Miles, suddenly feeling helpless. "Please go and tell my father what has occurred," I said. "I will bring Mother, and help you in the search."

Miles nodded, and just as easily as if our previous

conversation had not occurred, we seamlessly stepped into working together once again.

For now, this is going to take priority. And one thing that I cannot deny is that he could be incredibly helpful in locating Joan if she did decide to wander off for some reason.

I wrapped my arm through my mother's, and guided her to my father's study. I tried to assure her as we went, but she would not hear it. She could only worry about where Joan was and what could have happened...which only made my own fears worse.

"...yet to find her whereabouts, but I am confident that we will be able to locate her," Miles was saying as we approached Father's door to his study.

"That foolish girl," Father said. "If she has taken such leave of her senses as to think this was a good idea – she ought to have known it would get everyone in an uproar."

"I can assure you, sir, we will do all we can to locate her," Miles said.

Mother and I entered the room, and she dashed across to Father where he stood at his desk. Just as she had done with me, she buried herself against his chest and began to cry once again.

"What is this all about?" Father asked, turning a frustrated look upon me.

"I have little idea," I said. "All I know is that Joan and I were having coffee together a little over an hour ago in the drawing room. Since then, I have not seen her, nor heard where she might have gone. She gave no indication that she was going anywhere, or planning on it."

"That is not a good sign..." Father said, patting Mother's back as she continued to wail against him. "Joan is never quiet about her plans, which means she must not have wanted any of us to know she was planning to leave."

I frowned, looking over at Miles for help. "Are we *quite* sure that we can declare her missing already?" I asked. "Is it not entirely possible, even likely, that she has gone out with some friends and none of us were made aware? What if she did tell you, Mother, but you were distracted or have somehow forgotten?"

Mother stilled ever so slightly, and looked up at Father. "Well...I suppose that is a good place to start, isn't it?"

Father gave me a firm look. "Could you come up with a list of the friends she spends the most time with?"

I was not confident of it. Joan's friends seemed to change all the time, as inconsistent as those theater folk tended to be. "I...might be able to."

Father stepped away from Mother, pulled a drawer open, and slapped a piece of paper and a pen upon the desk. "Write away, then."

I swallowed hard, my mouth going dry. "Very well," I said, and sat down at the desk to begin writing.

It was difficult to come up with a list with Father looking over my shoulder, while listening to Mother's soft sobs in the corner. The immense pressure to get this right became almost too much to bear. I scrawled down a few names that I was relatively certain Joan still saw regularly, as well as a few others I had heard her mention more recently. At the end of half an hour, I had a list of a dozen names to present to Father.

"This is all you could come up with?" he asked.

"I imagine that if they do not know where she is, they might be able to direct you to someone who does," I said. "And it is getting late. The sooner we can reach these people to speak with them, the better." *And the sooner we can have this all behind us.*

Father scooped up the list. "Come on, then, Miles. Gather up the boys from the kitchen and I shall give them directions."

"Of course, sir," Miles said, following him from the room.

Father hesitated just outside the door and glanced back at Mother. "My dear, you must get on the telephone and ring up your own acquaintances, call anyone you can think of who might know something."

"Yes, of course," she agreed softly.

"I am going to go and search her room again," I said. "Maybe Joan left a playbill or something like it behind..."

I climbed the stairs to our room, feeling somewhat

guilty for leaving Mother behind. She had become so worried, so anxious so quickly. It unsettled me.

Perhaps I should have taken it all a bit more seriously, but I could not help but think that this could be easily explained and we were all nothing more than irrationally anxious after everything we had all been through.

Maybe this is why I am able to keep a level head about it, I thought. *I can see what they cannot. Miles equally seems calm. We have little reason to worry this soon.*

I pushed Joan's door open and strode inside. The stillness within should not have startled me, but it seemed as if it were beckoning me in. I turned on the floor lamp next to the door and crossed the room, just as I had hundreds of times before.

I had to resist the urge to whisper Joan's name. I knew that she would not answer, after all.

I walked around her bed, looking for anything that might indicate where she could have gone. Everything seemed in its place; her shoes remained in a neat row tucked inside her wardrobe. Her writing desk was empty, as usual. No playbill as I had hoped. No notes, no letters...just discarded scraps of paper.

I was not quite sure what I was looking for after wandering around for a few minutes. It looked as it always did, not a thing out of place. Which made me think that everything really was all right.

Unless...

Out of curiosity, and with as little fear as I would admit to, I crossed to her closet and slid it open. All of her suitcases sat on the top shelf just as they always did, untouched.

I did not know if that made me feel better or worse.

I descended the stairs a short time later, after taking a chance to peer into my room and the upstairs drawing room, as well as the bath. I wondered if she had somehow locked herself up in there after a quarrel with some new love interest that she had not yet told us of. But no, there was no sign of her.

I made my way to Father's study once again, and heard him and my mother speaking inside.

"Surely that must be it," Mother said. Her tears had stopped and her tone was steadier. "She talked of it so much."

"I should not doubt it..." Father said with a heavy sigh. "It would explain a great deal. She knows we never would have allowed it, but with your sister living out there, and with this new interest of hers in film acting, at least we know where her destination likely is."

With your sister living out there –

My stomach twisted, and I threw the door open.

"You think Joan has gone to California?"

Mother and Father both looked at me, startled by my sudden appearance. "That is our best assumption,"

Father said. "I am surprised we had not considered it before."

I blinked at them, staring back and forth.

"You do not remember her talking about this?" Mother asked. "It is a wonder I forgot until now, but she has made mention lately of wanting to go and visit my sister out in California, where she might be able to visit all those big theaters and shows out there. I believe she also had some idea of trying to get into moving pictures. You know how captivated she is by the new talkies."

"You think she ran away to try and get a part in a motion picture?" I asked.

"Would you put it past your sister to want to become a star or some such nonsense?" Father asked. He sighed heavily. "I do feel a great deal better knowing that she might have just finally given in to that flighty nature of hers and taken off."

"You aren't worried any longer?" I asked.

"I didn't say that," Father said. "But I do feel more confident that this might be what she has done."

"It's been some time since I heard her mention a desire to do anything like that," I said.

Mother shook her head. "Were you not listening to me earlier? She has been talking a great deal about wanting to take a trip, and this is the only trip that I can ever remember her talking of specifically. You said that she said nothing to you, correct?"

"That is true," I said. "I suppose she has mentioned travel recently, but...California?" I turned to Father. "What of her friends?"

"Most have been telephoned, and know nothing," he said. "Miles and some of the servants from the kitchens are out questioning others in person, but I doubt they will find her."

"Why?" I asked, my anger growing. "Why are you so certain?"

He gave a wave of his hand. "We shall wait to see what they bring back. I have already spoken to a friend on the police force, who suggests we give Joan time to surface with an explanation of her own, before filing an official report. Nonetheless, come the morning, I shall at least hire a private investigator to look into the matter."

"Hire someone? But Father, I could search – "

"No, absolutely not," Father interrupted, becoming suddenly stern. "You are not to get yourself tangled up in this. One daughter to worry about is more than enough. Am I clear?"

I did not know what to say. I could only stare at him.

"My private investigator will likely be heading out on the first train to California tomorrow morning," he said. "As such, the matter will be in good hands. I shall communicate with your aunt to look out for Joan's arrival, and we will have this whole affair resolved before the week is through."

I frowned, shaking my head. "I do not know if I fully agree with you," I said. "Why would Joan take the opportunity to go now? Today of all days? Would she not have chosen to go while I was away? There seem to be so many reasons why she simply would *not* leave right now and so suddenly – "

"Your sister is an impulsive girl," Mother said. "You know that. She makes decisions without much thought, and rashly."

"Yes, but Mother – " I said.

"No, Sylvia, I agree with your father about this," Mother said. "It makes the most sense."

"No, I truly do not think it does," I said, becoming more and more worried. The idea of her going to California concerned me, but not as much as the reality that something much, much worse might have happened to her...

Why am I so determined to think that something bad did happen, though? I wondered. I knew the answer. I had witnessed more than my fair share of ugly crimes. Experience now told me that if I worried something was wrong, it likely was.

Remain calm, Sylvia. Just a short while ago, you were the one who was not as worried, and now the tables seem to have flipped. It may all yet be well.

So I settled down in a chair in my father's study to wait. I waited for Joan to return home, first and foremost, expecting she would be back even before Miles returned. But the hours passed and I continued to stare at the same page in a book I'd plucked from a shelf, without reading more than a few sentences before my mind wandered and I had to begin again.

Seven o'clock came. That did not seem terribly strange, as early as it was.

Then eight o'clock. Then nine.

"How late do those plays of hers usually last?" I asked.

Father looked up from his newspaper, which he had been reading far too casually for my liking for the past half hour. "She typically does not return until after ten," he said, glancing at the clock. "But we have already established that is likely not where she is. We just need to wait for Miles' report before I send for the investigator."

I pursed my lips and buried my face behind the book once more.

Ten did come...and go. At half past, a commotion out in the hall sent my nerves singing. I sat up, practically throwing the book aside as I craned my neck to try and see out into the hall.

Miles came into the study, his expression apologetic. "Sir, I regret to inform you that there have been no sightings of your daughter anywhere in the city tonight, by any of her friends," he said, sounding somewhat breathless. "We checked with over a dozen people, some of whom sent us farther along elsewhere, but no one has seen her."

"Did you check the nearby theaters?" I asked, my heart beating uncomfortably in my chest, making my stomach ache.

He glanced at me, nodding. "She was not there, either."

*This is not good...*I thought. *One of those people should have been able to tell us where she is.*

"Then it must be as we thought," Mother said, sounding exasperated, shaking the sleepiness away as she stood to her feet; she'd been snoring fifteen minutes prior. "She must be well on her way to California. Likely halfway to the first station in Chicago by now."

"California?" Miles asked. "Is that where she has gone?"

"That is where everyone is supposing she went," I said, fear making goosebumps appear up and down the lengths of my arms. "I, however, am not convinced."

"Sylvia, we discussed this before," Father said, laying his hands flat upon his desk, frowning at me. "She has mentioned this, time and again – "

"But she was ill prepared for such a journey," I said. "All of her suitcases were still in her room. Do you really think she would have packed nothing?"

"She might have thought it rather romantic to go

without a great deal," Mother said. "You know how your sister is."

"She has more sense than you think," I said, growing more and more frustrated with the both of them by the minute. "Mother, I fear that something might have – "

"Your father said he was going to hire an investigator," she said, her own voice rising over mine. "He will look into it for us. We need not worry."

I could only stare at her. *Did she really believe that? Or did she simply not* want *to worry?*

"I cannot believe she would have left without any sign," I said. "There should have been something in her room to indicate a trip like this was on her mind – "

"All her talk of being bored and longing for an adventure of sorts must be the only sign she decided to leave," Mother said.

I glowered at her. "Mother, she knows your nerves, and would not be so irresponsible as to frighten you, or Father, or me – "

"She has little thought for anyone apart from herself," Father disagreed. "She has always had her head in the clouds, full of silly dreams. I used to hope you would influence her to be more sensible, but if you ask me, these dangerous crimes and investigations that you have taken the habit of involving yourself in have only encouraged the both of you to – to – "

I steeled myself, anger simmering beneath the

surface, feeling betrayal close at hand. "To what, Father?" I asked.

Miles eyed me warily, before looking back at my father.

"To behave foolishly," he said, doubling down on his disapproval. "I always told your mother, all the independence and reckless behavior we have so unwisely allowed would lead both our girls to no good."

I got to my feet, striding to the door. "You think this to be so foolish?" I asked, shooting a bitter look at him over my shoulder. "You shall see how foolish it is when I am the one to find her before your investigator does."

I yanked the door closed behind me, the *slam* satisfying right down to my core.

3

I stomped off down the hall, tears burning at the backs of my eyes as I made my way back to the parlor where Miles and I had been speaking earlier. I sunk down into the hideous, green armchair when I arrived and allowed the tears freedom as I wept for my family, for my sister, for the uncertainty of what was to come.

I had barely begun to collect myself when I heard a knock at the door. "Don't come in," I snapped. "I do not wish to see anyone right now."

I had expected Mother's voice, or even Mrs. Riley's. Instead, it was Miles.

"I brought you some tea," he said, his voice partially muffled through the wooden door. "I thought it might do you good as you plan."

I perked up. "...All right," I said, drying my eyes with the hem of my sleeve. "You may come in."

Slowly, he pushed the doors inward, and gave me a tentative smile as he appeared. "Are you all right?" he asked.

"No," I said with a disgusted snort. "Here I am, sitting here in self-pity when my sister could be – could be kidnapped, or injured or – " My voice hitched. "Or worse..."

"Well, I may not know anything about what is happening to her right now," he said, bringing a steaming cup of tea and setting it down in front of me. "But she is related to you, and there is an astounding resiliency in your family." He tried another smile, but I could not find it in my heart to return it.

He cleared his throat, sitting down on the arm of the empty chair beside mine. He interlaced his fingers, keeping a careful eye on me.

I noticed the scuffs on his typically polished shoes, as well as the flecks of mud along the hem of his trousers. *He really must have been all over the city, hurrying, trying to find her...*I realized.

"I know full well that this is not the time to return to our discussion from earlier..." he said. "But I want to offer my assistance to you, as I always have, in helping you to find your sister. I realize after everything that was said, you may very well ask me to stay out of it, and

I will, if that is your choice. I simply want to make the offer."

It did not take a great deal of effort to see the sincerity in his gaze.

"My father thinks me incapable," I said. "Thinks me *foolish* for all I have done..."

Miles said nothing.

I swallowed hard, looking up at him. "We must continue our discussion eventually, but I cannot deny that your help has been invaluable to me in the past," I said. "For now, I will once again choose to trust you. I cannot do this alone, and – and I fear that every minute will count in our search for Joan."

Miles nodded. "Very well," he said, and then slid into the chair properly. It seemed that my acceptance was what he was waiting for to stay with me there in the parlor. "So your father seems convinced that she has gone off to California, but you do not think so. Might I ask why?"

"It's rather simple," I said. "Joan is not a terribly mysterious person. I have never known her to keep secrets, at least not for long. She always tends to let something slip. I think she believes herself to be a great deal more difficult to read, hoping to be an actress in all ways, even in her personal life...but she never has been able to fool me. If she had seriously been planning on going all the way out to California any time soon, I am certain it would have begun as a wisp of an idea, a passing mention. Our parents would have talked her out of it, and then she would have turned it into a joke, whimsically dreaming of what it must be like out there, who she might meet. Once again, everyone would discourage the notion of her going so far away, and she would have dropped it."

"Right," Miles said. "And you are certain that is the only way she would treat it?"

"Let me give you another example," I said. "Many years ago now, the same sort of situation occurred. Joan got it in her head that she wanted to go and see the circus in New Jersey. She had seen a flyer downtown as we had been walking one day. Mother and Father disapprove of circuses all together; Mother cannot stand the way the performers fling themselves around so dangerously, she is afraid she is going to witness a death. But Joan became all the more determined to go...until one morning, we all awoke to the terrible sound of something crashing down the stairs. It ended up being her traveling case, which she had stuffed with feather boas and her gaudiest dresses."

"What if she grew wise from that experience?" Miles asked. "Maybe she realized that she would have to take greater caution?"

I shook my head. "My sister might be smarter than she was back then, but she has gained little grace. I know how unkind that sounds, but I highly, highly doubt she would have been able to sneak out of the house without anyone seeing her."

Miles' brow furrowed. "Which makes me wonder... It might be wise for me to question each and every staff member, to make sure they saw nothing."

"It would probably be wise, in case she bribed any of them," I said, an unsettling feeling growing in my chest. Why had I not thought of that before? "Regardless, I do not think she left with deliberate planning. When I went to search her room, everything was as it should be; clothing, traveling cases, shoes. Everything that a fashionable young woman like Joan would wish to take remained untouched. And as long of a trip as it is to California, there is no way she would have left without bringing at least some of it with her."

"That is a valid point," Miles said.

"I cannot remember the last time she left the house without making a fuss about having the *right* jacket or pair of gloves or hat to go with her dress," I said. "It is unheard of that she would have up and left with absolutely nothing, no matter how adventurous she fancies herself to be."

"Very well," Miles said. "For now, let's say I agree with you, as I believe you might very well have a better handle on your sister than even your parents do at this point. So, what can we assume has happened?"

"Of course, I do not wish to entertain the idea that something...something tragic has occurred," I said.

"Even saying it aloud, I have a hard time logically thinking of a situation that could have lead to that. It was such a short time since I left her that she went missing. I do think she left the house...but to go where?"

Miles shook his head. "It's difficult to know, given the fact that none of her friends were able to tell us where she was. The most recently that her friend Cynthia saw her was last Saturday, when they attended the opera together."

I frowned. "Those of us here in the house were the last to see her," I said. I scratched at my cheek, trying to go back over my discussion with her. "The one thing that I will agree with my mother about is that Joan *has* seemed to have been bitten by the travel bug. She has been wistful about going somewhere, but California was never mentioned to me. Not recently anyway. She wished that she had gone with me to Newport, but when I had invited her to accompany me, she refused it. I think she regretted that decision in the end, but I suppose she really has been wanting to go somewhere, to do something exciting."

I crossed my legs, looking down at my hands in my lap.

"I believe she wanted some excitement, because the last few months have been so full of strife," I went on. "I cannot blame her, not really. I fear that I have not helped her."

"You think she might have done something rash?" he asked.

"I have no idea," I said. "I wish I had been paying closer attention to her lately. If I had known – "

"There is no sense in wasting your energy on the 'what-if's', as it will do nothing apart from drive you utterly insane," he said. "It's best to focus your efforts on what you can control and see and remember."

I drew in a deep breath through my nose, trying to remain as calm as I could. "Yes, you are right," I said. "I suppose I will need to ask Mother about Joan's actions while I was gone."

"Now that you mention it, I believe I observed the same spirit of unrest within your sister as well..." he said, running his hands over the scruff of his chin. I had only just noticed it because he typically kept such a clean appearance.

"You have?" I asked. "What do you mean, exactly?"

"The same sort of longing," he said. "I, too, have heard her mention a desire to travel, to experience life...and I think you are correct that it is a result of all the turmoil recently."

"What has she said to you, in particular?" I asked.

"Nothing *to* me, but I have overheard her mention nostalgia a time or two," he said. "Missing friends, wishing to reconnect with people she has not seen in some time, much like she has seen you do."

My face flushed at the thought; my most recent

letter had been from the friend in London who had told me all about the murder of Miles' late wife. Perhaps it was best not to speak of that particular detail right now. "Anything else?"

"Nothing in particular, no," he said. "Nothing concrete, that is. Flippant remarks. She seemed... regretful. Almost lost in her own thoughts."

"I've thought the same," I said. I sighed, trying desperately to think back to our conversation. "She was jealous that I went, and wanted to have an exciting trip like I had. I imagine she wanted to be out of the city, just as I did."

"You did?" Miles asked.

I looked away. This was *not* the time to discuss the frustration between us. Not now. "What should we do?" I asked.

"Where else might she have gone?" Miles asked. "I doubt she would have gone all the way to Newport after you had just returned from there."

"I doubt it, as well," I said.

"Do you have family in any nearby cities or states?" he asked.

"We have a few," I said. "And our summer home further north...but she would not go there without any of us. There would be no staff to open up the house and no rooms prepared to be slept in. It would be freezing at this time of year. Even she would know that."

Miles nodded. "Still, it may be wise to go up there and look," he said. "Or at least to send someone up there to look."

"I suppose," I said. "Maybe we should suggest it to Father."

Miles nodded.

I sighed, sinking back against the chair behind me. "I am worried that Joan has been keeping something from me," I said. "She must have been. Keeping it from all of us, really. And I fear it is going to be to her detriment."

"She may have been, but there may also be a very simple explanation," Miles said.

I would have liked to believe him, but I had little idea whether or not it was the truth. If it was, then wouldn't Joan have come home by now? "Perhaps..." I said. "What should our next steps be, then?"

"The hour is late," Miles said. "It might be a bad idea to try and leave the house now."

A chill swept through me. "Are you suggesting we wait until morning?"

"I realize it is unsatisfactory, but consider the fact that there will be no one to speak with...unless you can think of someone we can question immediately?"

I crumpled beneath the truth of his words. "No," I said. "But we cannot just sit here! For hours!"

"I understand how difficult the idea of waiting is,"

Miles said. "Do you think it would be better to go out and search during the middle of the night?"

My first reaction was to say yes, that every second counted, but then my sense caught up with me. "No," I admitted. "Searching in the dark and cold is pointless, and could lead us to pass over something important."

It sounded as if I was making excuses, and I hoped more than anything that Joan was not suffering somewhere at that very moment...

I pinched my eyes shut, willing the images of her frightened and alone out of my mind.

"There must be something we can do," I said.

"I think you had the right idea earlier," Miles said. "We need a place to start first thing in the morning. We need a name that we can track down. Your mother may very well be the best one to talk to."

I nodded. "Yes...and perhaps without my father," I said. "He might do all he can to convince her that Joan has gone to California, and that is the end of it. He seems determined to believe that."

Miles nodded. "I can watch and make sure he has gone off to bed before we speak with your mother," he said.

I glanced up at the clock, my heart sinking. "It's almost midnight," I said.

"Then let us not delay any longer in speaking with your mother," Miles said. "And I will make sure there are a number of servants who remain awake this evening so as to receive Miss Joan if she does manage to wander home in the middle of the night."

That gave me a modicum of relief, but little else. "Very well," I said. "I can only hope Mother is able to help us."

"I imagine she will be of some help," Miles said.

He rose from his seat, and walked toward the door. He paused right beside me...so close that I caught the scent of the wood he had been carrying in to the parlor earlier clinging to him. "Are you all right?" he asked.

My eyes stung. "I'm...afraid," I said.

He raised a hand, extending it toward my shoulder...then paused before evidently thinking better of it. He lowered it as he strode past me. "I know..." he said.

I blinked, eyeing my shoulder where he had almost touched me. My skin prickled as if in anticipation.

"But we will find her."

"How do you know?" I asked.

"I know you," he said. "You do not give up. You have yet to fail."

Yet...I repeated in my mind. *I hope this is not the first time I do.*

4

The nightly routine of my family rarely changed. We would enjoy dinner together around seven, convene for tea and games at eight-thirty, and then would typically disperse to our own rooms by ten. It was a rare occasion that I saw my mother or father after that hour, though Joan and I would often stay awake talking until well after midnight.

This situation, as different as it was, still set my nerves on edge as I climbed the stairs to my mother's room. She and my father had rooms on opposite sides of the hall from one another, and while I passed by them frequently enough during the day, wandering down the corridor this late felt strange.

"It must have been ten years or so since I came to call on my mother this late," I said in a low voice to

Miles as we reached her door. "Last time, I was nothing more than a frightened little girl with a head full of bad dreams."

He gave me a surprisingly sympathetic look. "I should think you are not all together different now, as worried as you are about Miss Joan," he murmured.

It troubled me that he was keenly right.

I raised a hand, hesitating for a brief moment before rapping my knuckles against the door.

"Who is it?" Mother asked.

"It's me, Mother," I said, my lips nearly brushing the door. "May I come in?"

"Certainly dear," she answered.

With a hard swallow, I pushed the door open.

My gaze swept around the room, but I heard her before I saw her. A pleasant little hum filled the air, allowing me to locate her sitting at her vanity table. She hummed to her reflection as she tugged her brush through her auburn hair that so resembled Joan's. She glanced at me through the mirror, and smiled.

"What brings you here this late? Is everything all right?" she asked.

I did not quite know how to answer the question. Had she already somehow forgotten what had happened over the past few hours?

I heard Miles slip into the room behind me, staying near the door as I assessed the situation.

"I...I thought it might be obvious why I was here," I said.

Mother smiled at me again, setting her brush down as she reached for the perfumed hair cream that she used every night before bed. "Oh, my dear, if this is about Joan, then you need not worry your head about it anymore," she said.

Did I dare hope that meant what I thought it might? "She didn't come home?" I chanced.

"No, dear," Mother said, her face falling briefly. "Unfortunately not, but your father has talked sense into me and calmed my fears. I agree with him that she is simply on her way to see my sister in Santa Barbara. It is a lovely place, though I have not been in years. I have heard it has changed much, and very rapidly."

I tried to ignore the growing frustration within me about my mother's nonchalant attitude. How could she be so calm when Joan was missing still? She was her mother. I should not be worrying more about her than our own mother!

"Mother, have you received a letter from Aunt Lillian recently?" I asked, trying to continue as calmly as I could myself. It was a question that had come to mind while Miles and I had been talking, the only other means of a mention of California that might have slipped my attention.

"Well...no, I suppose I haven't," Mother said, massaging the cream into the ends of her long hair.

The room suddenly smelled of rose water and olive oil, which never failed to remind me of her. "That does seem a little odd, doesn't it? I wonder how they have been affected by the falling stock market. Your uncle has always been so brilliant that I should hardly wonder if they made it through untouched."

"Yes, but she has not written to you in the past few months?" I asked. "Nor telephoned? Not while I was gone?"

"No, dear," Mother said, finally turning around on her cushioned stool to look directly at me. "Why do you ask?"

"Because, Mother, as I said earlier, I cannot think of a time in recent memory that Joan has mentioned California," I said.

"Perhaps not to you, but she has always had it in her heart to go," Mother said. "She talked about it with me for a long, long time."

"Perhaps before she had the opportunities that she has had here in New York," I said. "The last time I remember her communicating a desire to travel out there was…it must have been three or four years ago."

Mother's brow furrowed. "It could not have been *that* long," she said.

"It was, Mother," I said. "Which is why I think you and father are mistaken."

Mother's gaze became distant for just a moment before she fervently shook her head, swinging herself back around to face her mirror. "No, I think your father is right, dear," she said. "She is likely comfortably asleep on a train, well on her way. She must know that your father will be none too pleased to have to foot the bill for her travel expenses, but at least we will know that she is all right."

I had to grind my teeth together to prevent myself from lashing out at her.

Out of the corner of my eye, I noticed Miles smoothing my mother's bedding, turning down the covers for her for the night. She did not even seem to notice his presence in the room, which I supposed should not surprise me. This was his job, after all. It only made sense that he would tend to his tasks, even at this hour.

I had to swallow my tongue. If I became angry with Mother, even mildly so, she would clam up and not speak to me any further.

I glanced at Miles, who I found watching me with a sidelong look, as well. He gave me a brief nod before turning to fluff my mother's pillows.

There was information I needed. Mother would have to deal with her own denial once I found Joan, and hopefully she would learn to trust me after this was all said and done.

"How was...how was Joan while I was gone?" I asked. I hoped that my tone sounded morose enough to convince her that I simply wished to discuss Joan because I missed her and cared for her. "Was she all right?"

Mother sighed, turning back around on her stool. "Yes, I suppose she was all right, though she has seemed rather distant," she said. "I think she is a bit heartbroken, you know."

My eyes narrowed. "Heartbroken?" I asked. "By whom?"

Mother's brows arched like the wings of a sparrow taking flight. "She never told you?" she asked. "There was a young man who walked her home one day. I was briefly introduced to him... Oh, what was his name?"

I stiffened. A romantic interest? And I knew nothing about him? I chanced a look at Miles, who had now begun to fold up the crocheted blanket at the foot of Mother's bed in case she wished the extra warmth during the night. The wrinkles in his forehead told me that this was news to him, as well.

"Do I know him?" I asked her, hoping to help her along.

She wrinkled her nose, shaking her head. "No, but your father did not care for him in the least after looking into him. He said that he was an utterly worthless fellow with a poor reputation and few suitable connections, and generally not worthy of her attention." She gave a nod. "I could not have agreed more. It is like Joan, though, to accept the attention of men without a great deal of means or standing.

You know she is not terribly sensible about such things."

"What did he look like?" I asked.

"Oh, he was certainly handsome, which is why she liked him, I assume..." Mother said. "About as tall as your father, with mousy brown hair and a pointed chin."

That was not much to go on. "Any distinctive features?" I asked.

"Well, I suppose there was that scar across his forehead, right near his hairline," Mother said, tracing the same spot with her own finger. "Rather nasty, but he seems to hide it well enough with hats, your sister says."

My stomach dropped. "She has been seeing Ned Baldwin?" I asked.

Mother brightened. "That's the name, yes!" she said, then she scowled. "Oh, he is a dreadful lout, according to your father."

"And father would be right," I said, my skin crawling. Joan was seeing *him*? Him, of all people? "I've heard nothing good of him – what in the world was Joan thinking?"

"Why do you think she up and left, my dear?" Mother asked. "She knows that she's made a mistake, and has taken off to deal with it on her own terms."

My mind began to race as quickly as a spooked hare. How could Joan have been silly enough to spend time with Mr. Baldwin? The rumors about his criminal associations were common knowledge. Besides, we had seen how he had treated a friend of ours, Madeline, how he had lied to her, broken their engagement, and then left for another woman without a word of apology. What could Joan possibly have seen in him?

"Do you know if they saw each other again?" I asked. "After he walked her home, that is?"

"I have no idea," Mother said, shaking her head. "To be honest, I had hoped that you might know more about it than I, and were simply keeping your sister's confidence."

I shook my head. "No, she said nothing to me."

I had experienced betrayal in my life, especially in the more recent months. People I had trusted had failed me, and those I thought I could depend upon disappointed me. I had seen up close and personally just how unreliable people could be.

But this sting was unfamiliar to me. *My own sister keeping secrets from me like this...*I thought.

It would not, therefore, surprise me if Joan *had* continued to see Baldwin, even after my father specifically forbade her from doing so, given how quiet she had been, how elusive.

*Maybe she snuck off with him...*I thought with a cannonball sized weight landing in the pit of my stomach. *Not to California...but to where?*

"I know you are worried about your sister, dear..."

Mother said. "We all are. But I have faith that she is well, wherever she is. I hope you can find some rest as we wait to find out what we can about her."

"Right..." I said.

Mother stifled a yawn as she finished tidying her hair.

"Well, I suppose we should both be off to bed," she said, getting to her feet. She glanced at the bed and smiled up at Miles. "Ah, Miles. Thank you so much. You are always so efficient and thoughtful."

Miles dipped into a bow, and stepped from the room.

Mother looked at me again, and I thought I caught a glimpse of a brief flash of fear, but it was gone quickly. "Try to get some sleep, won't you?"

"I will try, Mother," I said.

"Good," she said. She crossed to me, took my head in her hands, and kissed my forehead.

"I love you, my dear," she murmured. "Sweet dreams."

"I love you, too, Mother," I said. "And you as well."

I slipped from her room, the door barely making a sound as I latched it behind me. I breathed in deeply, allowing my mind a chance to catch up with everything I had seen and heard.

"She is worried, you know."

I jumped, my heart shuddering within me as if I had been struck by lightning. "Miles..." I said, leaping away from the door, my hand clamped over my thundering heart. "I did not see you."

"My apologies," he said. "I thought you might want to discuss what she said in there."

"Yes," I said. "But away from their rooms. I do not want Father knowing I went in to speak with her. Not yet."

We made our way back down the hall and toward my own room. When the door was closed behind us, I let out a long, heavy sigh.

"As I said, she is worried," Miles said, folding his arms. "She is trying her best to hide it, but she is not entirely convinced Miss Joan has gone to California."

"I know," I agreed. "In fact, I think she is putting on a show to keep herself from falling apart. She hopes that Father is right, but I think hearing me worry makes her all the more uncertain."

Miles nodded. "And this Mr. Baldwin... Who is he, exactly?"

"He's nobody," I said, and to his puzzled look, I went on. "Truly. We have mutual acquaintances or I would know nothing of him at all. He is a young man who hovers around the edges of high society, pretending to be one of us, seeking opportunities to profit by any connections or information dropped before him, yet I believe he finds little success. He has no particular family that I know of. He has never made anything of himself or pursued any real career. I have heard rumors that he associates secretly with criminals, collecting debts owed them by the wealthy."

"Sounds like a charming fellow," Miles said, his nose wrinkling.

"He is the furthest from it," I said. "Lately, he likes to meet young ladies of means in hopes he can charm one into marrying him. A rich wife, I suppose, would support him for life. He fooled a friend of ours once, but upon learning her father intended to give her no money if she married him, he left our friend. It was despicable."

"Clearly," Miles said. "But this is a good thing, you know. This means we have a lead."

I looked up at him, my eyes widening. "You're right..." I said. "I was so angry about the very thought of him that I had not realized we now have a name to follow."

"And he was not one of the people on the list you wrote earlier, either," Miles said. "Which means we have yet to go and check into him."

"Excellent!" I said, striding toward the door. "Then we must be off – "

"Just a moment, Miss Sylvia," Miles said, stepping between me and the door. "You must remember the hour."

I glanced at the clock; it was now nearing one in the morning.

My heart sank.

"Our lead will still be there, first thing in the morning," he said. "As difficult as that is to hear right now, I understand."

I sighed, nodding reluctantly. "It is difficult, but what can we do? We cannot hope to find where he lives in the middle of the night, and there would be no one we could ask, either. We might be in a panic because Joan is missing, but that doesn't mean anyone else is..."

I glanced at Miles.

"...Though I will say that I am tempted to go and speak with the police again," I said. "Maybe Father's friend did not think the matter serious, but someone else in the department might."

Miles shook his head. "Perhaps if she remains missing long enough, they will involve themselves. But in the meantime, you and I can solve this problem more quickly than anyone. We have a vested interest in finding her, and you know all the parties involved. The police do not."

"That is true..." I said. My heart sank. The idea of suffering through an entire night of fear seemed like an acute form of torture that I did not want to endure.

"You need rest," Miles said.

I laughed hollowly.

"I shall bring you some warm milk," he said. "It will help calm your nerves."

"I doubt anything will be able to calm my nerves," I said. "I will likely spend the next few hours watching the clock, hoping that Joan is still alive when we finally find her."

"We have no reason to think that anything violent has happened to her," Miles said.

I gave him a weary look. "There is nothing to say that it hasn't, either."

He drew a deep breath. "It will not do to allow your mind to wander in that direction," he said.

"I know," I said. "But that does not mean I will be able to stop it."

He nodded. "Then I will remain here and sit up with you, if you like."

"You do not have to – " I said, but then stopped myself. "Very well. I suppose it will be better not to have to suffer through it alone."

"Good," he said, and walked to the chair at my writing desk. He turned it around and took a seat. "Then I shall stay."

I could not explain why knowing that he would be there gave me some calm...but within the hour, I had fallen asleep in the thickly cushioned armchair that I settled in, my head lolling back against the headrest.

5

I managed to sleep for a solid five hours. Six o'clock came, and as the sun peeked through the drawn curtains in my room, I roused from the exact same position that I had fallen asleep in. When I sat up, I rubbed my neck, which ached from the crooked position I had slept in.

"Good morning," Miles murmured from the chair at my writing desk. He looked as put together as he had the night before. One would never have guessed that he had been awake the entire night.

I blinked away the sleep, my mind foggy...until the whole day before crashed against me like a tidal wave.

Joan.

Her face pressed against my mind, filling my head with memories that moved so quickly that I could not keep up with them.

I cradled my head in my hands, my breathing sharp and piercing. I gave myself a moment to let it pass, trying my best to soothe the fears and worries with logic and reassurances. *We are going to look for her today. We don't know that anything bad has happened. There is little reason to think we won't be able to find her.*

"Are you all right?" Miles asked.

I shuddered, my breathing ragged. "I...I think so," I said.

"The morning panic is always the worst," he said. The numbness in his voice made me want to ask how he knew that, but I did not have the strength.

"Here," he said, reaching for a tray resting beside him on the desk. "I have already brought up your breakfast. Take as long as you need to eat and dress, and meet me down in the foyer."

"I – " I said, my mind whirling. "Thank you."

He strode toward the door, eyeing me over his shoulder. "And make sure you do eat. We could be out the rest of the day without another chance to have anything. You will need to keep up your strength."

"Right..." I said, even as my stomach recoiled at the idea.

I dressed easily, and ran a quick comb through my hair, thankful that my stylishly short locks did not require any time to arrange. I managed to choke down the egg and muffin, both of which tasted good enough that I snatched up the glass of milk and downed it in three long draws. I had not realized how thirsty I was.

I hurried down the stairs half an hour later, just before seven.

"Very good," Miles said, stepping away from his post along the wall near the door. "Are we ready to go?"

"Yes," I said.

"Where shall we start?" he asked, holding out my thickest winter cloak.

"The theater where Joan spends most of her time," I said as he helped me shrug it on.

"Good thinking," Miles said with a nod, pulling the door open for us.

"I have no idea where we might find Mr. Baldwin, nor any idea of who we could ask apart from someone at the theater," I said.

"Do you think someone would have a connection to him there?" Miles asked, making his way down the stairs ahead of me, holding out his hand to help me on the icy, bottom steps.

"We can only hope," I said. "We don't have Joan to ask, after all."

He helped me into the car and we were on our way. "I hope your father won't be too upset with my absence," he said, glancing over his shoulder. I could see the exhaustion in his face, pulling at the skin beneath his eyes.

"I wrote up a quick note to leave my parents, letting

them know I would be out for most of the day," I said. "I intentionally left it vague enough that they would not have many questions for me. I think they will suspect I am frustrated about Joan and want some space."

"And you said I would be driving you?" he asked.

"Indeed," I said. "They will be pleased that I have taken you, as Mother asked me recently if you had done something to upset me."

Miles said nothing, but the tension in the air told me that he had clearly heard me. He knew as well as I did that I had been upset with him, and I had been avoiding him lately.

We did not speak again until Miles needed directions for how to reach Joan's theater. I gave them to him and tried my best to set my frustrations aside once again. I had agreed to allow him to help me, hadn't I? Then why was I acting so sheepish now?

I frowned as we drew nearer, wondering what we might find.

"These are the beginning steps," Miles said. "We are that much closer to finding her."

"We have learned nothing yet," I said.

"Yes, but we are on our way to doing just that," he said. "This is where the search really begins."

His words encouraged me, and I straightened slightly. *Maybe before the end of the day, even,* I thought, though I knew that might be far too much to hope.

We reached the theater, and after climbing out of the car, I looked up at the brick building that stood in a quieter part of town that had yet to be greatly developed. I often spent a great deal of time down here waiting for Joan to finish her practices or dress rehearsals. I had read many a book while sitting on the steps leading back to the dressing rooms.

"My best bet is that this is where she met Mr. Baldwin," I said, crossing my arms as we gazed up at the building, side by side. "She would not have been introduced to him at any of the social functions my parents would attend, nor would she have met him through any of her friends recently, as rumors about him have begun to swirl."

"I thought you said you knew of him through your friend that he left," Miles said.

"Yes, we share acquaintances but none likely to introduce him directly to us," I said. "His reputation is questionable, his family is of no renown, and he has no suitable occupation." I glared at the building's doors, wondering how much danger had befallen my younger sister because of this place. "This would be one of the few logical places where they would be able to meet."

"Who should we talk to?" Miles asked. "Is there a director, perhaps, who might know the ins and outs of this place?"

"I can only assume," I said. "Apart from some of the actors, I am not familiar with many of the staff."

He gave me a sidelong look. "Well? Are we going to go in as ourselves? Or should we recreate one of our old personas?"

"I think it would be unwise to try and pretend to be anyone else," I said. "There are going to be people here who will recognize me, and who have met me."

"Right," Miles said. "And as you are looking for your sister, I imagine people will be more willing to help you."

I stiffened beside him. "Yes, that is true. I am not going to hide my intentions here."

"So when this news reaches your father, he will know you have stood your ground," Miles said, and an appreciative grin spread across his face. "Good."

"Let's get inside," I said, pulling my cloak more tightly around my shoulders. "I cannot afford to freeze out here."

We made our way to the main doors at the theater, and I knew that we would not have come too early, as the theater often opened at six for early practices. There was more than one time where Joan had to be there before seven for a ten o'clock performance. The doors were unlocked, and even as we stepped into the main entrance, the sounds of theater life could be heard.

A saw worked somewhere nearby, likely on the main stage through the trio of double doors at the far end of the foyer, the sound bouncing off the massive auditorium. A woman with a rather flat voice sang from down the right hallway, and a man with a rumbling, deep voice hollered something which was quickly answered by another.

"Rather busy for a Thursday morning," Miles said. He looked around and pointed to a display of signs with arrows near the main doors. "Here we are. Director's office, to the right."

"Off we go, then," I said.

We started down the hall, passing by a girl with a full peacock tail and a man lumbering past carrying what seemed to be a real set of armor. The director's office was at the very end of the hall, with a large, red star painted on it.

Miles knocked, and we waited. And waited. And waited.

"I don't suppose he is in yet," Miles said.

I sighed. We had already run into a dead end. "Well, we could always wait until he arrives – "

The door opened, revealing a much shorter, rounder man than I had expected to find. His balding head shone from the light of the lone lamp sitting upon the desk behind him. He pressed his glasses up his face, squinting hard at me. "Can I help you?"

I blinked at him. "Are you the director?" I asked.

"Theater manager, but I suppose I do a bit of directing, too," he said. "I run this place. Why? You here to pitch a play or something?"

"No, sir," I said. "I was hoping that you could help me."

He squinted even further. "Help you? With what?"

"Are you familiar with one of your actresses, a Miss Joan Shipman?"

"Shipman...Shipman..." he said. "Can't say that I am. Why?"

I swallowed hard. "Well...she is my sister, and – "

"Ah, I don't take family recommendations for casting," he said, holding up a hand to stop me. "I'm sorry, but you'll have to go through auditions just like everybody else."

"No, that is not why I am here," I said. "My sister is missing, sir, and I was hoping you could – "

His eyes snapped open at that. "You aren't accusing *me* of anything, are you?" he asked. "My word, this is the third accusation in the past year! I don't have anything to do with the cast off property. Besides, I don't even know who this sister of yours – "

"Sir, it is nothing like that. We are merely trying to find her whereabouts," Miles interrupted, stepping in for me. "We have no cause to accuse you of anything... unless you wish to give us a reason?"

"No," the theater manager said. "No, of course not."

"Then may we ask you some questions, then...Mister...?"

"Mr. Henry is fine," said the man. "Look, I don't really have a lot of time. I've got a rehearsal in an hour with a live horse carriage, and then around two, I've got a painter coming to look at the foyer. If this is going to be a long talk, can we schedule it for some time later this week?"

I could only gawk at him. Had he heard nothing I had said? Later this week could be too late!

"It really would be best if we could speak now," I said. "It will not take up much of your time, I assure you."

"Fine," he said with a loud harrumph. "What do you need?"

"We are looking for the whereabouts of someone who might know where my sister is," I said. "Are you familiar with a Mr. Baldwin?"

He shook his head. "Never heard of him. Is he an actor?"

"No," I said. "But I am concerned that my sister met him while she was here – "

"If he's not one of mine, then I surely won't know who he is," he said. "Next question."

*This is not going nearly as well as I had hoped...*I thought. "Very well," I said. "What of my sister? Has she been around here in the past twenty-four hours?"

"I have no way of knowing," he said.

"But you are the manager," Miles said, brow furrowing. "Surely you know – "

"There are a dozen rehearsals going on here at a time," he said. "Not every actor makes it to every one of them, and I don't make the directors keep lists of those in attendance. To be honest, I don't really care if they miss half their rehearsals, as long as the final production looks good."

"So there is nothing you can do to help me?" I asked, frustration growing within me at a rapid pace.

"I don't know what you want me to do," Mr. Henry said. "It isn't as if I can pull the information out of the air, can I?"

"No, but you could certainly do more in terms of at least wanting to try," Miles said. "A young woman is missing, and you are being entirely unhelpful."

"What do you expect me to be, the police?" he asked. "Just because the girl might act here once in a while doesn't mean I am her personal caretaker. I'm sorry, but if you really want information, you should go talk with some of the other actors and stage hands. They might be able to help you. If you'll excuse me, I must be on my way."

He ushered us out from in front of his door, promptly closing and locking it. He disappeared down the hall, without another look back at us.

"That could not have gone worse," I muttered. "I have never been more discouraged during an investigation."

"Maybe it was a bit of a long shot to expect him to know every little thing that goes on in this theater," Miles said. "Though I imagine some of the people on the list you gave me yesterday include the actors Miss Joan knows here?"

I nodded.

"Right, and they did not know where she was, when previously questioned," Miles said. "None of them had seen her recently."

I sighed. "Joan said that she hoped her theater group was going to come up with some sort of plan for the spring," I said.

Miles stiffened, looking at me. "She said that?"

"Well, yes," I said. "Why?"

He snapped his fingers. "That is even more proof that she had no intention of going to California," he said. "Why would she be looking forward to seeing her actor friends if she was going to be gone?"

"Maybe it was meant to throw me off," I said.

Miles shook his head. "I don't think your sister would be quite so deceitful," he said. "And, if we are honest, I do not know if she would have had the cleverness to think that far ahead."'

"You're right," I said. "Then she likely had no plans to leave the city."

"Exactly," he said.

"All right..." I said, some of my confidence returning. "But where are we going to go from here?"

Miles scratched at his chin. "I suppose we could keep asking around here if anyone knows anything about this Mr. Baldwin."

"Mr. Baldwin?"

I looked up to find a tall, languid sort of man, whose face was as long as Mr. Henry's had been round.

My heart skipped. Had he heard me correctly? "Uh, yes," I said. "Do you happen to know him?"

"The young Mr. Baldwin?" he asked. "Rather charismatic lad?"

"I believe so," I said.

His brow furrowed, and he looked more like a lion than a person. "What do you need with him?"

"I think he might know where my missing sister is," I said.

He pursed his lips. "I could provide you with a rough idea of his whereabouts, but he's been known to move around a great deal."

"You know where he is?" I asked. "How?"

"I'm the theater manager's assistant," he said. "And often the administrator. Mr. Baldwin has done some work for us in the past, though none of it was quite up to my standards..."

It seemed too good to be true. "Would you be willing to share with us?"

"I would...if you tell me who your sister is."

I swallowed hard. "Joan Shipman," I said.

His eyes widened slightly. "I hope you can find her..." he said. He turned to the office across from Mr. Henry's and stepped inside. He found a scrap of paper and began to scrawl an address down.

"Do you know anything about the pair of them?" I asked.

He shook his head. "I know nothing, unfortunately. I have met your sister once or twice, but I did not know that they were acquainted. That man seems to be following after another young actress every week." He shook his head. "I would like nothing more than to ban him from the premise for all the trouble he causes, but I don't think Mr. Henry would refuse entrance to anyone who buys as many tickets as he does, no matter his intentions."

I frowned. That was certainly not encouraging. "Well, thank you very much for this."

"As I said, I hope you find her," he said. "I wish I could be of more help."

"This is very helpful," I said. "Truly."

Miles and I started back toward the foyer. "That could not have worked out any better for us," he said.

"I am relieved," I said. "I thought we were going to have to speak to a dozen more people before we found anything. Maybe we can still find her before..."

"It really would be best if you did not allow your imagination to wander," Miles said. "We should – "

"Joan?"

An icy, biting chill gripped my heart. I whirled around, my eyes sweeping the foyer. They fell upon a girl who must have been around my sister's age.

"Oh..." she said, her eyes widened. "You are not Joan."

"No, I am not..." I said.

"I apologize for mistaking you for someone else," the girl said with a nervous chuckle. She was quite striking, apart from the gap between her front teeth. She brushed some of her pale blonde hair out of her eyes. "Have a good day – "

"No," I said, reaching out to stop her as she started past us. "Did you mistake me for Joan Shipman?"

The girl's eyes widened further, and a rather late smile blossomed on her face. "Y – Yes, I did," she said. "Do you know her?"

"Yes," I said with a nod. "She's my sister."

"Oh, is she?" the girl asked. "Well then, I suppose it is little wonder that I mistook you for her." She giggled into her hand, a dozen or so gold bangles tinkling on her wrist.

Mistook me for Joan? That surprised me. I could not remember the last time someone had mistaken me for her, or the other way around. Then again, most of the people we knew had known both of us, so there was little reason for confusion. This young woman could not have known Joan terribly well, as there were quite a few physical distinctions between me and her. My stomach twisted, the knots tightening. "Are you a friend of hers?" I asked.

"Oh, yes, most certainly," the girl said with a fervent nod.

"I apologize that we have yet to be introduced," I said. "My name is Sylvia Shipman."

"Oh, what a pleasure to meet you," she said. "I'm Miss Fiona Jacobs."

No, that name is not familiar, I thought. Not even remotely. "The pleasure is all mine," I said, putting on as kind a smile as I could. "So, did you two meet here, at the theater?"

"It is a funny story, really," Miss Jacobs said. "We did meet here, but through a mutual friend. I am not an actress, not in the slightest. I am simply guilty of coming to all of Joan's more recent performances in the past few months. She's absolutely astounding, don't you think?"

Her eyes had widened so much that they were nothing but perfectly round, gleaming orbs filled with an almost crazed awe.

"I suppose that I have had the pleasure of watching her for most of her career," I said. "And spent a great deal of time rehearsing with her."

Miss Jacobs' mouth fell slightly open. "That is...just amazing. I would have loved to have seen that."

"I do not know if you really would have, if you had seen us," I said. "Just out of curiosity...when was the last time that you two saw one another?"

The girl tapped her chin with a slender finger. "It is

funny you ask," she said. "Yesterday afternoon, in fact. We had lunch."

Yesterday afternoon?

A whirring started in my ears, and I stared at her with a fright that I had not known I could have. *Wait... yesterday afternoon?* I repeated in my mind. When had I been sitting with Joan? Could it have been just before she and I had sat with each other in the parlor that she had lunch with this girl?

"Did you?" I asked. "Oh, how wonderful. You see, Joan has been so longing to spend time with her friends. I went away for a few weeks and I think she was wishing that she had joined me."

"Oh, that is terribly sad," the girl said with a pout. "The poor dear, I am glad that we had the chance, then."

"Did she...say anything of interest when you two were dining together?" I asked.

The girl blinked at me, her eyes wide once again. "Interesting? Hmm...well, I don't know. I suppose she did tell me about a recent meeting she had with a talent scout. A fellow who was supposedly looking for the next big star, or some such."

A talent scout was not particularly interesting to me, though I supposed he would be to Joan. *And again, here we are with more evidence that she would have wished to have stayed in the city. Why would she run if she had another opportunity lined up for her?*

"That...isn't quite what I meant," I said with a smile.

Her mouth formed a distinct *O*, and she gasped. "Oh, do you mean a *love* interest?" she asked. Then she shook her head. "I am sorry to disappoint you, but she said nothing about that."

I shook my head. I had that information from Mother, but it was good to hear that she might have already moved past Mr. Baldwin. "Not quite that, either. Did she say anything about a trip? Or perhaps traveling?"

Her expression changed, becoming visibly worried. She took a step back away from me, looking back and forth between Miles and I. "Did something happen?" she asked.

Oh dear... Was I too obvious in my questioning? I wondered.

"Is she – is she missing?" she asked.

That question struck me upside the head as if she had physically done so. How could she guess that?

"Oh, my goodness – she seemed entirely fine when we were having lunch," the girl said. "There was nothing – at least, nothing that I could see that was wrong..."

I gave too much information away. Why did I not want to tell her what I knew? Why was I afraid to tell her that Joan was missing?

Because she thought I was Joan... I didn't want to upset a friend of Joan's.

"I'm sorry," I said. "I did not mean to take up so much of your time... Please, excuse us."

I turned on a dime and hurried off toward the door. The footsteps behind me were familiar, and I knew that Miles was following.

"Are you all right?" he asked in a low voice as we strode out into the cold.

I was already growing tired of hearing him ask that. "No...no, I am not all right," I answered flatly.

"I thought not," he said, and he opened the door to the car for me.

6

"Let us be on our way," I said. "We do not have any time to lose."

"One moment, Miss Sylvia," Miles said after he had climbed into the front of the car. His warm breath cast clouds of fog on the front windshield. "Did anything about that conversation seem odd to you?"

I glanced out the window once more at the theater, thankful we had managed to find some of the information we had come for, but regretful that we still felt no closer to Joan. "It was incredibly strange that she mistook me for Joan," I said. "I cannot remember the last time that happened, if it ever has."

"Yes, that was rather bizarre," Miles said. "But that isn't quite what I meant."

I eyed the steering wheel. I had yet to hear the

sound of the engine turning over. "Miles, why aren't we going yet?"

"We will," he said. "Think, Miss Sylvia. What did that girl say that was strange?"

"I don't know, Miles," I said, glaring at him. "I do not have the patience for playing games like this. Why don't you just tell me what you are thinking?"

He gave me a patient look despite my frustration. "Was it not strange that she was one of the last people to have seen your sister, apart from you?"

I hesitated. He was right. That did strike me as strange, even worrying. "Yes...but I managed to see Joan after her. At least I believe so, based on when she and I had coffee together."

"I do wonder if that young woman was not entirely honest with you about what she and your sister discussed," Miles said. "If Miss Joan was planning to go anywhere, I cannot imagine she would have been behaving all together normally."

I frowned. "She was with me, at least for the most part." I scowled, shaking my head. "If only I had been paying closer attention to her, I might have been able to catch that something was wrong and intercepted her before anything happened."

"Miss Sylvia, do not lose yourself in the possibilities that never were and never will be," Miles said. "It is a dangerous path to wander down, and you will regret that you ever gave yourself the chance to do so."

I did my best to quell the intensity of my thoughts. "You are right," I admitted.

I glanced at my jeweled wristwatch. It was nearing eight o'clock.

"Yes, we should be on our way," Miles said. "Do you have the address?"

I handed it up to him.

We started down the street at a slow pace, and had to stop only two blocks away when a slew of traffic appeared. Everyone seemed to be starting their days.

"I do wonder if that Miss Jacobs knows more than she was letting on," I said. "Seeing Joan so close to her disappearance... Though I suppose it really could have just been lunch, and she was as oblivious as I." I frowned, nervously twisting the gold watch around my wrist. Father had it specially made and engraved for my last birthday. "I have never heard Joan mention her name before. They must be newly acquainted. As such, how could I expect someone who hardly knows Joan to know something was troubling her?"

"I would not expect it," Miles said. "Though, she did perhaps give us a lead..."

"How so?" I asked.

"The talent scout she mentioned," he said. "He was on Joan's mind, it seems. I wonder if he has some connection to all this."

I straightened, my heart quickening. "I had nearly forgotten," I said. "That seemed to concern her, you are right. A talent scout..." I repeated, thinking. "My word, that would not be the first time that she had hoped to secure the interest of someone influential in the theater business, but does this mean she managed to impress one of them?"

"That could mean a great deal of change for her," Miles said.

"Yes, and none of it good, likely..." I said. "My father will not hear of her taking part in anything more serious than the occasional small plays."

Miles was quiet, but I noticed his grip tighten on the steering wheel.

"What are you thinking?" I asked.

"It does make one wonder if she knew precisely what you just said, and decided to take the next steps all the same," Miles said.

I shook my head. "Even she would not be foolish enough to defy Father like that."

"Would she not?" Miles asked. "Is that something she has always wanted, the opportunity to turn her passion into a career?"

I hesitated. "She loves acting, I know that much," I said. "But would she choose that over her family?"

"She would not be the first person to be tempted by fame and fortune," Miles said. "Especially if this talent scout offered her a reasonable deal. She could see it as her way of leaving her mark."

"Why would that matter to her?" I asked as Miles

took the next right to try and escape some of the main roads that were packed with traffic.

"Think about it," Miles said. "With the investigations you have been involved in, you are doing important things. It would not surprise me if she felt somewhat left out, wanting to do something equally significant."

"I...have never thought about that," I said. I didn't know if it made me feel any better or any worse, really, but it did shed light on something I felt suddenly incredibly ignorant about.

"I am not saying it is certain what has occurred, but this talent scout may be worth speaking with, if things do not pan out with Mr. Baldwin," Miles said.

"Yes," I said. "That is a good point. Oh, I wish I had the sense to have asked Miss Jacobs about his name..."

"I imagine there will be other ways to find out who it is," Miles said as we came to yet another stop at a busy intersection. At this rate, it would take us an hour just to move halfway across town. "Do the theaters not have connections with certain talent scouts or agents?"

"I honestly do not know," I said. "I imagine they would."

"It must be quite like how bankers work with certain brokers they trust," Miles said.

"The way Joan has described it, theaters are territorial," I said, crossing my arms. "They have distinct areas that they pull actors from, and once an actor makes a name for themselves at that theater, they often don't jump around."

"That makes a great deal of sense," Miles said. "Which leads me to believe they would have the connection to this talent scout Joan met."

"I can only hope she did not schedule a meeting with them without someone else knowing," I said. I sighed. "I suppose at the very least, I could track down Miss Jacobs again and see if *she* remembered the name of the scout...though this is all starting to feel a great deal like a wild goose chase."

"I can understand why you feel that way," he said. "With almost every other case, you have not had such a close connection...apart from your uncle, that is...with the – "

"Please don't say victim," I said, my stomach turning over.

"I'm sorry," he said. "I didn't think that through."

"It's all right..." I said.

Silence swept through the car like a cold breeze, and I could think of nothing apart from Joan...dead. I could hardly stomach the idea, it terrified me straight through to the marrow of my bones. It did not help that I continued to imagine various ways in which she could have died, or been killed.

I tried to swallow but my throat ached. What if she...was gone?

I had not wanted to consider it, still didn't, but

knew that if I did not allow myself the chance to consider the possibility, then how much of a wreck would I be if it ended up being the truth?

If she – if she was gone – I could barely stomach the thought. It would be so horrendously unfair that I had left her side unknowingly to tend to my own matters, only to find that if I had just delayed, had maybe given her more of my attention when she had made it seem as if she wanted it after my two week absence...

*There is little use berating myself...*I chided myself. *It will do nothing to change the situation if it's true. It might have already happened. I cannot change the past.*

I had watched people lose their family members multiple times in the past few months, watched families grieve over the loss of their loved ones. I had witnessed the death of my uncle, violent and extreme as it was. Yet that could not compare to this...not in the slightest.

It felt as if part of my heart had been ripped from my body, carved out with a blunt knife.

I gave myself a moment to feel it, *really* feel it as if it were real...because for all I knew, it could be.

"Miss Sylvia?"

I looked up. Miles had turned almost all the way around in his seat, and we were stopped. We had pulled off to the side of the street, in front of a long row of plain brick buildings. One seemed to be a dilapidated factory of some sort, and beside it was a strip of rowhouses, all of which had seen better days.

"I'm sorry," I said. "I suppose I was lost in my thoughts."

"We are here," Miles said, gesturing out the window. "Judging by the state of this place, we may not be terribly far off the mark in regards to this man being suspect. It certainly does not look like the address of a reputable person."

A trashcan stood near the lamppost, overflowing and spilling into the street. I did not have to look far to spot a broken window. A car backfired on the next street over.

"I think you are right," I said. "I know that one is not supposed to judge based on appearances alone... but if I had any idea that this was the place where Mr. Baldwin resided, I would have told our friend to chase him off when she first met him."

Of course, Miles himself was living in much rougher circumstances the first time I laid eyes on him, I remembered.

I sighed, shaking my head.

"All I can hope is that we can find some answers," I said. "I should like to be several steps closer to Joan by the time we leave."

"We can only hope, I suppose," Miles said. "But you have been through this before. There are a great many possibilities, and often times, we do not find what we are looking for right away."

"Maybe this time will be different," I said.

Miles did not seem convinced. He glanced up at the house. "You said that he knows you?"

"I highly doubt he will remember me," I said. "Unless he also thinks that Joan and I resemble one another."

Miles smirked at that, but the expression quickly faded. "Shall we allow that to play to our advantage?"

"No," I said. "I want him to know I am her sister, and that I am looking for her. He will feel the weight of that, if I can help it."

"Very well," Miles said. "Then you have my full support in it. Are you prepared to go?"

"As ready as I believe I shall ever be," I said. "How can one prepare for this sort of thing?"

"By practice, I'm afraid," Miles said.

"Every moment we waste could lead Joan that much deeper into danger," I said. "We cannot delay."

Miles nodded. "Then let us go and meet our new friend, shall we?"

7

I walked toward the door with my chin held high. If I was to face someone who might have had a hand in my sister's disappearance, then I needed to do so with dignity and grace. He could not be allowed to see me tremble. I would not give him the satisfaction of seeing me afraid of him.

Miles walked up the front steps ahead of me, casting wary glances at me over his shoulder. This was a necessary encounter, though greatly unwanted. I should not even be here, should not even be inter-acting with this man, yet what choice did I have?

Miles knocked on the door, and stepped back as we waited. I checked my wristwatch once again; half past eight. An early hour to be calling, certainly, but this was no time for courtesy.

"Perhaps he is not home," I said, discouraged after a five minute wait that felt like an eternity.

"Or still sleeping," Miles said, leaning back and gazing up at the windows above us. "It is quite early."

"Try again," I said.

Miles obliged.

Still no answer.

"What should we do?" I asked.

Miles knocked for a third time.

A crash sounded from somewhere up above us, followed by a string of shouts that I found myself rather glad I could not understand clearly. Footsteps stomped through the house, and soon reached the landing behind the door.

I stepped back behind Miles as the door flew open...and Mr. Baldwin was standing on the other side.

"What could you possibly need at this hour?" he snapped, looking back and forth between Miles and me.

He was not nearly as handsome as I remembered him being, though I supposed that had a great deal to do with the situation in which I found myself. He had fiery red hair that sat too long at his shoulders, partially pulled out of his face. His thin face reminded me of a bird, especially with his small, watery eyes and underbite.

What could Joan have possibly seen in him?

"Good morning, Mr. Baldwin," Miles said. "We appreciate your presence."

"Yes, well, it wouldn't have been me, if my servant was any good at his job," he muttered under his breath. "I'll ask you again; what do you want?"

"We are here to ask you some questions," Miles said. "Might we come in?"

Mr. Baldwin crossed his arms, leaning against the doorframe. "No, I don't think you will," he said. "I never entertain before noon. If you would be so kind as to come back then – "

Miles thrust his foot in between the gap of the door and the doorframe just as Mr. Baldwin began to shut it. I winced for him, as I could not imagine it being without pain. "Sir, if you would just give us a moment of your time – "

"See, now you're just being rude," Mr. Baldwin said, a single pale, blue eye staring out through the gap in the door. "I tried to be kind, but you are overstepping your bounds. I should call the police."

That was the very last thing we needed at the moment. "Mr. Baldwin, do you not recognize me?" I asked.

He turned his eye toward me, and eased the door open enough to get a proper look at me. "Are you suggesting that I should?" he asked.

"I suppose I should not expect you to, as we only

saw one another in passing once," I said. "My name is Sylvia Shipman."

His expression did not change. I wondered if he had even heard me.

"Joan Shipman's sister?" I asked, chancing another time.

He blinked. "And?" he asked.

It was my turn to look blankly at him. "Are you acquainted with her?"

"What does it matter to you if I am?" he asked.

Why is he being defensive? I wondered.

"Sir, we have come to ask you some questions about your relationship with Miss Shipman," Miles said.

"Who are you?" Mr. Baldwin asked, his brow furrowing.

"My name is Miles. I am the family butler, and – "

He let out a bark of a laugh. "Then I have nothing to say to you," he said.

"Sir – " Miles said.

Mr. Baldwin interrupted him. "The butler...coming to speak for the family. My word, I thought the Shipman name was worth something. I suppose I was wrong." He laughed again.

Anger bloomed in my chest, burning red hot, so intense that I wanted to reach out and grab him by the collar of his shirt and shake him until he stopped cackling. "Mr. Baldwin," I snapped, raising my voice. "My sister is missing, and I have recently learned that the two of you were in a romantic relationship."

His laughing slowed, and he wiped the corner of his eye. "Oh...is that the rumor now? No, she was nothing to me."

"That is not what I heard," I said. "I heard that the two of you were seen talking together, as you walked with her home."

He shrugged. "And I am not allowed to behave as a gentleman on occasion?"

On occasion?

"Mr. Baldwin, what is your connection with her, then?" Miles asked. "And when was the last time you saw her?"

He shrugged again. "Am I supposed to account for every moment of my life?" he asked. "I can hardly remember what I had for dinner last night. How can you expect me to tell you about all my social engagements over the past weeks?"

"Have you seen her recently?" I asked.

He turned to look at me, his eyes narrowing. "You are persistent, and I do not particularly care for persistence," he said, his teeth clenching together. He rolled his shoulders, and his expression smoothed.

"Mr. Baldwin, my sister is missing," I said again, trying another tactic. I allowed some of my fear to seep into my voice, hoping that it might stir sympathy in him. Anger, it seemed, was not working. "I am looking everywhere for her, and asking everyone she knows. You are someone that I learned she recently started spending time with, and I hoped – I hoped that you might be able to help me."

He lifted his chin high, staring at me down the length of his nose. I sensed a swelling pride, as if I had finally found my place. "Oh, she's missing?" he asked, looking away. "What a pity."

I stared at him, stunned. Had he really just been so nonchalant about it? Did he truly not care?

"I'm sorry, is this somehow amusing to you?" I asked. The question slipped from my lips before I could remember that it might not be the wisest idea. "My sister's absence is worthy of nothing but sarcasm?"

He raised an eyebrow at me, and his expression darkened like a storm cloud passing over the city. "I have nothing to say to you, nor do I owe you, or her, anything."

"Do you truly care so little for the wellbeing of another person?" I cried. "A young woman that you cannot deny knowing – "

"I can spurn whom I well please!" Mr. Baldwin said, straightening up, his chest expanding. "I am surprised you feel bold enough to question me when I have already given you my answer."

I opened my mouth to lash out at him, but I lost my balance as a force tugged me backward down the steps.

I snapped my head around to find Miles pulling me down the stairs, back toward the car.

"Wait!" I cried. "No – "

"Come away," he hissed under his breath. I noticed a bright flash in his eyes as he pulled the car door open and practically shoved me inside. He took little care not to slam it after me, either.

He joined me once again from the front seat, and it was not ten seconds before we were driving down the road again.

I whirled around in the seat and pressed myself against the window, only to catch a glimpse of Mr. Baldwin still standing upon his stoop, watching us go. "Miles, why did you – "

"You were about to make the situation a great deal worse for us by provoking him into calling the police," he said. "I understand that you are upset, that this is entirely personal, but – "

"How was I going to make it worse?" I asked, equally as hotly. "He was only bluffing about the police. I was trying to find the best way to get him to talk!"

"He was not going to talk," Miles said. "And he likely never will, no matter how you approach him."

"But why?" I asked. "And how could you possibly know that?"

Miles sighed heavily, easing his foot off the gas pedal; we were flying down some of the less traveled streets with a bit too much speed. "There are, unfortunately, some people in this world who relish being difficult. Obstinate. I quickly realized he was one of those, and watched as he enjoyed your suffering."

I furrowed my brow. "Enjoyed it?"

Miles nodded, his expression grim. "There are those who find it, as you said, *amusing* to torment others and frustrate them. They live for the thrill of the fight. Those are the sort of men who belong on a battlefield, where those idiosyncrasies might be pruned out of them."

"Idiosyncrasies..." I muttered under my breath as I sank back against the seat. "That's a very kind way to put it."

"You do know what I am trying to convey, though," he said.

"I have never met a person like that in all my life..." I said.

"I certainly have," Miles muttered. "Perhaps it is a difference of origin, but I have met a number of people who rather enjoyed ruffling the feathers of those they knew, purely for the fun of it."

"It's sadistic, is what it is," I said.

"Yes, well, that is why I don't think we would ever get anything useful out of him," Miles said. Once again, we found ourselves at an intersection buzzing with cars; we had rejoined the major parts of the city, the veins by which the inhabitants traveled through its body.

"But what if he had something to do with it?" I asked. "Now we will never know."

"He might have," Miles said. "Though it seemed that he could not have been any less interested in her or her fate."

Her fate...I tried to swallow, but my throat was dry.

"How in the world are we going to find Joan now?" I asked.

"Try not to allow yourself to panic, Miss Sylvia," Miles said as an opening in the traffic allowed him to squeeze in between a taxicab and a sleek, new car in deep black. "There are still other options."

I straightened. "Oh, I had nearly forgotten. The talent scout."

"Right," Miles said. "I think the best thing we can do is set Mr. Baldwin aside for the time being – "

"I am not ready to write him off, yet," I said quickly.

"Nor am I," Miles said. "But I do think pursuing other options could be productive as well, and perhaps even lead us to Miss Joan. We might be able to circum-navigate Baldwin all together, if he really did know anything."

I thought back to Mr. Baldwin's short, vague answers, and the sneer he wore as I had nearly grov-eled at his feet. He could not have been any less helpful...or any less of a monster in regards to how he spoke about Joan.

Maybe Miles is right...I thought with a twinge of disgust. *Maybe I would have made matters worse if I had offended Mr. Baldwin enough to report us to the authorities. It would derail the investigation so thoroughly that I would surely be too late to find Joan before –*

"I am sorry that he was exactly what you thought he was," Miles said. "I wish that he could have had a bit more compassion toward you and your family."

"It is of no matter," I said, frowning. "I knew the sort of man he was going into the encounter, and he simply proved my opinion of him to be true. He is a scoundrel, through and through, and I will joyfully share that information with any and all who ask it of me. If I have my way, he won't be able to find a young woman to give him any attention in the entire city."

Miles nodded. "Seems a fair enough solution."

"What do I care if he was unkind to me?" I asked, knowing now that I was lying to myself. "It matters not how he treated me. I am still going to find Joan, whether or not *anyone* helps me."

"You will not be doing this alone," Miles said. "I am going to stand with you the whole time. We will find her, before it's too late."

His resolute tone gave me a burst of hope. *I won't have to do this alone*...I thought. That was what I needed to hear, especially in the midst of how alone I truly felt.

"Thank you, Miles," I said. "I am not sure I deserve such support."

"Yes, you do, and much more..." Miles said, and then fell silent as a car came barreling out of a side street, its headlights glaring right at us as it hurtled toward us.

8

I had always heard that when an accident occurs, those involved, if they live to tell about it, describe the event as seeming to happen very slowly. The idea always terrified me, considering what might occur, what it would feel like in that moment. There was no preparation one could make, not even in one's mind. When accidents happened...they always happened when least expected.

The headlights from the car coming straight toward us flared brightly. All I could see were the pair of them. Nothing else stood out to me, apart from how large, how round, how golden they were –

The air, frigid and biting, seemed still, as if in anticipation of what was to occur. If I held my breath, I imagined that time itself could have stopped entirely.

All I could think was one thing...about one person...

Miles...

A blare of a horn. A shudder of the car. A shooting, crashing pain in my forehead as it bounced off something cold and hard –

I blinked, my vision blurring. The car careened to a stop, and my whole body nearly slammed into the seats in front of me.

"Are you all right, Sylvia?"

Miles' frantic words pierced through some of the fog in my mind. "I – I don't know..." I said.

I reached up to feel my tender forehead, and winced as pain shot through my entire head.

The front door flew open and banged shut, and a moment later, the door beside me flew open, and Miles was there. He came near to me, his face tremendously close.

He took my head in his hands, surveying my forehead with squinted eyes. "You were injured..." he said. "I am so terribly sorry – "

"It's – it's fine," I said. "It isn't your fault, you weren't the one who nearly hit us – "

"Wait here," he said, and departed from the back seat once again.

My mind whirled as it tried to put together the pieces of what had happened.

Miles reappeared with a handkerchief balled up in

his hands. "Here," he said, gingerly leaning back in to me and pressing the cloth to my forehead. It was immediate relief, and soon the cool feel of packed snow began to soothe the bruises that I knew were inevitable there. "This should help with any swelling that might happen."

"Thank you..." I said.

I glanced through the front windshield, and noticed that we had parked near the library a few streets from my family's house. "Did we pull over after all that?" I asked.

"Yes," Miles said, bent over beside the car, peering in at me. "I managed to avoid the accident, but I admit that it was a bit of a violent reaction."

"It's all right..." I said. "It is certainly preferable to wrecking the car."

"I was far more concerned about you than the car," Miles said.

"Everything is all right, though?" I asked. "Are you injured?"

"I am fine," Miles said. "I only wish I had warned you to hang on, or brace yourself, or something."

"It all happened so fast," I murmured. "I – I am grateful that you were quick thinking enough to avoid the other vehicle."

He eyed the handkerchief pressed against my forehead, and his face slackened. It was clear he was not comforted by that, not particularly.

"Shall I take you home so Mrs. Riley can take a look at your head?" he asked.

"No," I said. "It's sore, but I'll be just fine."

"Are you quite certain?" he asked, stepping back.

"Yes," I said. "Finding Joan is far more important than some spot that is not going to heal any faster if I am home than if I am out here with you."

"I am simply worried that it might be worse than it looks, and you might need to have it examined more closely," he said. A car honked loudly as he tried to squeeze between our car and another waiting to turn left going the other direction. "You might be so nervous that it is numbing the pain."

"That may be the case," I said. "But that does not mean I want to give up the search yet and abandon Joan. I realize we are no closer to finding her, but what if I did take the time to go all the way home and spend what would end up being the rest of the afternoon at the house? Then we could not come back out until after dinner, and that is if Mother would even allow me to leave at all."

"I see your point," Miles said. He eyed me warily once again, as if I might crumble to pieces right there if he dared look away from me. "All right. Then shall we be on our way?"

"Yes," I said. "I would not wish to waste any more time."

He returned to the front of the car, and we started

off again. I could not deny that fear was indeed playing a factor in my reactions right now. Fear of what happened to Joan, fear of the way Mr. Baldwin treated me, and now fear of our car nearly colliding with another vehicle –

If that had happened, would I be dead by now? Would it have killed me instantly?

I shivered, and swallowed hard as I looked at the window I had probably struck my head against. I tried not to imagine the glass shattering into hundreds of pieces, likely because I would have gone through it. Car manufacturers really ought to install some sort of safety harnesses to hold passengers in their seats at such times, I thought fleetingly.

"You wished to return to the theater, yes?" Miles asked.

"Yes," I said, clearing my throat as well as my thoughts as best I could. "I would like to find this talent scout, and see what he might have known."

"Certainly," Miles said. "I am hoping it will be a more profitable trip than our last one."

And anything to get me out of the car as soon as possible, I thought with great apprehension.

We reached the theater just as it was nearing eleven. I had not realized just how long we had pulled off to the side to check my head for injury, nor how long it had taken us to drive back across the city. I had not noticed that Mr. Baldwin's house was so far from where we lived. It made me all the more grateful that he was almost as far away from me as he could possibly be.

The theater buzzed with activity as we entered the building. Much like bees in a busy hive, workers flitted this way and that, up and down the halls, in and out of the auditorium, each with his or her own tasks.

A young man teetered out from the hall carrying almost a dozen paint buckets, all of which swayed dangerously in his arms. Miles stepped out to help him, but not before they all toppled to the ground, rolling away from him. The poor boy sagged, and looked as if he were about to burst into tears as we turned away and headed down toward the theater director's office.

I did not have a great deal of confidence that this would go well. After how unhelpful the director had been when we were here earlier in the day, I suspected he would be just as indifferent now. Perhaps he would even be annoyed that we had returned so soon.

"How is your forehead?" Miles asked, looking at my face once again.

I gingerly touched the spot. I had abandoned the handkerchief in the car, dumping what little was left of the snow out onto the sidewalk before we came inside. "Sore," I said, then frowned. "How does it look?"

Miles' nose wrinkled slightly. "It would easily hide behind those fashionable fringes some women are fond of these days, where the hair sweeps across the forehead," he said, moving his finger across his own forehead in a crescent shape.

"That is all well and fine, but what does it look like?" I asked.

"It's already a shade of purple…" he said.

I sighed. "I should expect nothing different." I gestured toward the director's door. "It is not going away. We might as well get on with it."

Miles nodded, stepping up to the door.

When he knocked, I was astounded to find it opening almost at once.

"I'm sorry, but I was just on my way – oh, it's you two again." The director looked back and forth between us, and as I expected, his eyes fixed on the blooming bruise on my forehead. "What happened to you?"

"It doesn't matter," I said. "Mr. Henry, I really must speak with you. I know that you are quite a busy man, and I do not wish to interfere with your work by any means, but it is of utmost importance. Please."

Mr. Henry sighed, removing his round glasses and rubbing his eyes. "You were here about your sister earlier, weren't you?"

"Yes," I said. "As I told you before, she has gone missing, and we have been all over the city trying to find out where she might have gone."

He regarded me with a steady stare that was

surprisingly patient. "Still missing, you say? And you said that she was one of my actresses?"

"Yes," I said. "She has been performing here for the last three or four years, I believe."

He nodded, and turned to look over his shoulder, and then glanced down at the stack of playbooks in his hands. His face softened ever so slightly, and he turned back and started toward his desk.

I glanced hopefully at Miles, and he looked equally surprised. He gestured for me to follow first, and I did just that.

"Go ahead and take a seat. Make yourselves comfortable," Mr. Henry said with a wave over his shoulder, not bothering to look at us. He had busied himself with a cabinet in the corner, pulling files from it. "You said your name was...Stewart?"

"Shipman," I said. "And my sister's name is Joan."

"Joan, yes," he said. "Thank you."

Miles pulled a stack of books from a chair and pulled it out for me to sit in. The rustling of papers was the only sound for a few moments before Mr. Henry laid a file out on his desk.

"Yes, I do have a file for her," he said. "I have tried to keep a record of every person that has ever performed here, and it seems that even if I have not kept up on them as thoroughly as I should have..."

"Do you remember her, then?" I asked.

He shook his head. "No. Unfortunately, I do not

have the luxury of remembering them all. The ones I do know are those who perform for me regularly, typically with larger roles."

"Is there anything in her file that might help us?" Miles asked.

"That is what I was wondering, but I don't suppose there is..." he said, replacing his glasses. He squinted down at the paper. "Unless you think that her association with any of the other actors might help."

He passed me a sheet with a list of other cast members who had performed alongside Joan, and I sighed. "I know all these names," I said. I looked at Miles. "These were most of the people that you or my father have already spoken with."

Mr. Henry sighed. "I am sorry. After you left this morning, I felt badly about how little I helped."

"Well, there still might be something you can help us with," I said. "We are looking for a particular talent scout that Joan might have met recently."

His brow furrowed. "A talent scout, you say? That is a possibility, as there are a number I am acquainted with."

My heart stirred. *Could it be that we are finally finding a lead?* "Would any of them have had the chance to meet any of your actors and actresses here?" I asked.

He nodded. "There are only two that I have allowed to scout from my plays," he said. "So I imagine its one of them. Do you know the name of the person your sister met with?"

"No," I said, internally kicking myself once again for not having the answer. "And I have very little information, apart from the fact that she met with him recently."

"No other description?" he asked.

"Well, according to our source, he is looking for the next big star," Miles said.

Mr. Henry's eyes lit up. "Ah, then I can almost guarantee its Mr. Beecham that she met with," he said.

"How can you be sure?" I asked.

"That is something he always says, that he is looking for the next big star," Mr. Henry said. "He has yet to discover them, as he tends to choose those who have far less experience than most, hoping that he can find a diamond among the rocks. Though I suppose it would be simple enough to ask the other scout I know, as well, in case I turn out to be mistaken..."

"How can we reach this Mr. Beecham?" I asked, sitting at the edge of my chair, ready to rise and be on our way.

"He should be around this evening for one of the performances," he said. "I would give you the address to his office, but he is never there, and as such, it would be a waste of time. He is sure to be here this evening, though, and you can speak with him then. Tell him that I have sent you to him, and he will be sure to listen."

I nodded, though I felt disheartened. This evening? That meant we had to wait hours before exploring our next lead. I did not particularly like that, knowing that the next few hours would be filled with gnawing worry and incessant looks at the time, but what else could we do? "Very well," I said. "Then I suppose we will just have to wait until this evening."

"I must caution you," Mr. Henry said as I rose from my seat. "Mr. Beecham is a bit obsessed with his work. He may well change the subject when you speak with him, and attempt to recruit the pair of you as clients. He has been known to do that."

"Really?" I asked.

"Yes. He looks at every person he meets as an opportunity," Mr. Henry said.

"Thank you, Mr. Henry," I said. "We will have to keep that in mind."

"Oh, and one more thing..." he said. "Your sister, I see, was recently in a play called *Silent Sea,* yes? I have heard tell of a couple, a young man and woman, who have been hanging around the theater a great deal, particularly before and after every show. Maybe they would know something."

"That is good to know," I said. "We will have to look into that." It might be a wide stretch, especially if they hadn't been around in some time. *That play ended in the middle of December, didn't it?* It had been weeks now.

"Certainly," Mr. Henry said. "I hope you are able to find her. I would be glad if you asked her to come and introduce herself to me properly when she is ready to return to acting."

"Yes, of course," I said. "And thank you."

The smile he gave me was sadder than I would have wished. "Take care, Miss Shipman."

We left his office and started back down the hall.

"Well..." Miles said. "Perhaps we should make our way back to the house. This would give Mrs. Riley a chance to look at your head."

"And a chance for my mother and father to question how in the world it happened," I said with a frown. "Though I suppose we have nothing else to do right now – "

"Did you find her?"

My heart skipped at the urgency of the question, and I turned to see the theater's assistant director, the tall, lanky man with a lion-like face we had met earlier. "No," I said.

"We are back looking for more information," Miles said.

"Oh..." he said. "Did things pan out with Mr. Baldwin?"

"No," I said. I didn't feel right telling him about the horrendous encounter we had with the man.

"Well...I should tell you that he has been here a great deal during some rehearsals lately," he said. "He has been doting on your sister, bringing flowers and candies for her all the time. Another young woman sometimes accompanies him."

"You know that for certain?" Miles asked.

The assistant nodded, his mane bobbing. "I think your sister quite liked it, too. It seemed a bit excessive to me, but I suppose that doesn't matter, does it?"

I glanced at Miles, and the puzzled expression he wore must have matched my own.

"And that mark on your forehead..." the assistant said. "Did that happen during your investigating today?"

"In a way," I said.

"Here, come with me," he said. He swept into a room near the end of the hall.

We followed him and, at once, I knew that the space was a spare dressing room. A stack of slender boxes sat on the vanity, all labeled with a shorthand I didn't quite understand.

"Go ahead and take a seat," he said.

"What are you going to do?" I asked.

"Fix it up for you," he said. "Not medically, of course, but I can hide it...if you would like."

My eyes widened. "That would be perfect, yes," I said. I promptly sat myself down on the stool, and he began to deftly apply a layer of what felt like paint to my skin, and then a layer of powder on top of it. I hardly ever made up my face, and it felt strange to have someone else do it for me, especially in such a specific way. I knew that Joan often talked about makeup being a crucial part of the stage productions, as it helped reduced glare from light and accentuate features, but this seemed different.

"Here we are," he said, holding up a small mirror and handing it to me.

I gazed at myself and blinked a few times. I had managed to catch a brief look at the bruising in the window of the car, and even then it had been rather distinct. Still...I wondered if Miles had not been making more of it than necessary.

"My word..." Miles said, stepping around to get a proper look at me. "He's erased it all together."

I gaped up at the assistant. "Sir, you might very well have saved me a great deal of inconvenience this afternoon," I said, thinking of the arguments I would surely get into with my parents if they saw such a mark.

He grinned. "Well, I am pleased to do so. I know it is not much, but I cannot imagine a young woman as lovely as yourself desiring unwanted stares from passersby." He set the mirror down. "Oh, and a mixture of lavender and warm tea will help that bruising heal more quickly."

"Thank you," I said. "That is very helpful."

"It is something I must know, given that our actors

rely a great deal on their skin looking their best," he said, tucking away some of the brushes and rouges that he had brought out. "I have had to learn a thing or two about concealing and healing, both."

"Well, thank you," I repeated. "It was very kind."

"I do hope you find your sister," he said. "I should like to see her back here again, safe and sound."

"I am certain that she would want nothing more," I said, a knot in my throat.

We departed a short time later, stepping out into the cold once again.

"That was a surprise," I said. "Mr. Henry was more sympathetic than I expected, given how impatient he was when we came earlier. And the assistant – I didn't get his name, did you?"

"No, unfortunately," Miles said.

I reached up to touch the makeup on my forehead, but Miles pulled my hand away from my face.

"Don't touch, it will smudge," he said.

"It's starting to itch, a bit," I said.

"If we are returning home, it will be best to keep it on for as long as possible," he said. "Though I am sorry that it's uncomfortable."

I sighed, lowering my hand. "It could hardly be worse than what Joan must be dealing with right now..."

"I know..." Miles said.

I was grateful that he did not try to correct my trajectory, even for a moment.

"I wonder about Mr. Baldwin," I said, not allowing myself to wallow in worry for too long. "I mean, about what the assistant said, as well as Mr. Henry."

"Yes, I found that terribly interesting as well," Miles said. "Is it possible that they have mistaken Mr. Baldwin for someone else?"

"I doubt it," I said. "Mother said that it was he who had walked her home, and who Joan had been so recently enamored with. Why is it that he acted so entirely monstrous to us when we spoke with him directly, yet it seems that he might have been completely obsessed with my sister when in public?"

"It does seem strange, doesn't it?" Miles asked. "I don't know... Something about it makes me uneasy."

"Me as well," I said. "There must be a reason...but why? Why would he want to appear infatuated with my sister, even so much so that she believed it herself, yet be so horrendous about her to us?"

"I don't know," Miles said. "But you are right. There must be a reason for it."

"What must be true is that his affection for her was never real in the first place," I said. "That much was clear when we met him. All of the gifts, all of the doting must have been nothing more than an act."

"But why?" Miles asked.

"I cannot guess," I said. "We need to get to the bottom of that."

"Maybe," Miles said. "Or maybe that has nothing to do with any of this, and perhaps he was spurned by her. Maybe we are searching behind the wrong doors."

"It's possible," I said. "I suppose not every person in her life could be tied to her disappearance."

"Our next avenue of investigation must be the talent scout," Miles said. "And I hope that we find we have been worrying after her for nothing."

"As do I..." I said. "Though, if we have been, she is going to receive quite an earful for what she has put us all through."

9

Miles insisted on taking me home for the rest of the afternoon. I told him that I would much prefer spending time out in the city, looking around, not simply sitting on my hands...but he worried that my head might only get worse as the day went on, and wanted me to have some time to rest.

I felt relief when we returned home and found that my parents had stepped out for lunch with a friend. It amazed me that they could have such a carefree afternoon, but I could not blame them...not entirely. I swallowed my frustration and allowed them to have their fun if they so wished. I would find Joan without their assistance. At the end of it all, we all wanted Joan to come home, safe and sound. At this point, it mattered little to me how it happened, or who managed to find her. I just wanted my sister back.

Miles brewed me up a pot of strong coffee. "The stronger, the better, for headaches," he said. "And if need be, we can apply some salve to the injury... though that would certainly ruin the makeup."

The coffee helped, though the dull pounding behind the bruise made it difficult to think. The longer I sat in the parlor, the more difficult I realized it might be to get up again and return to the theater. Every muscle in the left side of my body had tightened and stiffened so thoroughly that it became difficult to turn my head. My wrist ached when I twisted it just right, and I could not quite close my thumb all the way.

"Some injuries only appear after you've had a chance to rest," Miles said, bringing a bundle of ice in for me to hold against my shoulder, which had also begun to bruise without my notice. I must have slammed it against the window at the same time my head bounced off the glass.

"I cannot afford to end up bedridden," I said. "We have to return to the theater this evening."

"Do you think you are up to it?"

"Yes," I said, ignoring the protesting of my muscles. "I am. I have no choice, Miles. I have to go."

He nodded. "I know," he said. "Your sister needs you."

"My sister needs both of us," I said, getting up from

my chair. I had to walk, to stretch my legs. "I cannot do this without you."

I managed to get dressed alone, refusing Mrs. Riley's help; she could not know that I was suffering as greatly as I was. If she saw my body dappled with bruises, she would send for a doctor and cause a great fuss. I winced and groaned my way through it, but I chose a dress that took minimal tying in the back or buttoning. Thankfully, the plum dress had a bit of give, and I was able to pull it on over my head. Paired with a thick pair of wool stockings and boots, I knew that I would not only be warm enough, but my injuries well concealed. I managed to wrap my sore hand in some bandaging before sliding gloves onto both hands.

After one last glance in the mirror, I found myself satisfied with my appearance. It was not nearly as formal as Joan would typically ask of me on any other night we were going to see a play, but it was simple enough for any acquaintances I might meet to pass me over. Inconspicuous and practical, the perfect disguise.

I winced as I started toward the door, the simple motion like tearing the very muscles in my arm.

*We did not even end up in an accident, and still I am suffering as if we were...*I thought as I started down the hall once again. I hoped my gait appeared normal; the last thing we needed were questions from some of the servants.

Miles met me in the foyer, raising his eyebrows in

question as I descended the stairs.

"I'm fine," I said with a smile. I heard Mrs. Riley's voice down the hall scolding one of the cook's assistants. "Let's be on our way, shall we?"

"Oh, Miss Sylvia, I hoped I would catch you," Mrs. Riley called after me just as I stepped up to the threshold of the front door.

My heart sank as I turned to her. I hoped more than anything that the makeup the man from the theater had applied would hold up beneath her scrutiny. "Yes?" I asked.

"Your mother is hoping you will be home for dinner this evening," she said. "I believe, despite her efforts not to think of it, that she is distressed over your sister's absence. Your presence may help to calm her nerves."

I could see the strain in the housekeeper's face. I knew how difficult my mother could be in the best of times, and since Uncle Walter's death, she had been inordinately in denial as well as prone to fits of tears. "I should like to be, but I am going to a play," I said.

Mrs. Riley's brow furrowed. "Now of all times?" she asked.

My face flushed. "I have had tickets for a long time, and I am...meeting someone there," I said.

Suspicion deepened the wrinkles in her forehead, but all she said was, "Very well, Miss Sylvia. I will let her know."

"Thank you," I said. "I shouldn't be out too late."

I felt a slight pang of guilt, as she turned away and started down the hall. The last thing my family needed to worry about was my own whereabouts this evening.

"Everyone will understand when we find Miss Joan," Miles said as he joined me, drawing the front door closed and locking it behind him. He pocketed the key and offered me his arm as we started down the steps.

"Maybe I should have explained the truth to Mrs. Riley," I said.

"It was a partial truth," Miles said. "We do hope to see someone at the theater. Anyway, she probably already suspects your actions have something to do with your sister." He pulled the door of the car open for me. "Housekeepers are more perceptive than people realize, and Mrs. Riley is even more so than most."

I looked around at him. "You don't suppose she will tell my parents, do you?"

"No," Miles said. "She knows how that will distress them. There is little use in such a thing."

"I suppose you're right," I said. "Oh, I just cannot wait for this to all be over with."

Miles nodded, but the strain in his face made my nerves flare up again. He worried about the same thing that I did, which was that it would not end well.

Maybe then I do not truly want it to be over...for then I

will have to deal with the reality that Joan might be – that she might be –

"Now, would you wish for me to accompany you inside?" Miles asked. "Or is this something you want to handle on your own?"

"I would like you to be there," I said. "I may need someone to talk sense to me, if I lose my temper again, as I did with Mr. Baldwin."

He gave me a wry smirk in the rearview mirror. "I hardly believe you will do anything like that again. I cannot imagine you would despise the talent scout as much as you did Mr. Baldwin."

"No...I suppose not," I said.

The theater appeared busy, but it was not nearly as busy as I might have expected for the night of a play. I had no idea if it was opening night or not, but the number of people indicated that this play must not have been one of the best attended.

"Well, with a name like *Circus Crimes,* I can see why the audience might be a bit scarce," Miles said as we entered the foyer.

I nodded, but found that my nerves had returned, buzzing within me like the hum of a string quartet warming up. These chases we had been pursuing all morning had left me feeling rather hopeless. That, coupled with the aches of my shoulder, my head, and my neck with every step, made me see little reason to hope for any success in meeting with the scout.

"How do we find the talent scout?" I asked. "I should have asked Mr. Henry about where and when specifically we could expect to find him."

"I think we can likely ask anyone that works here at the theater," Miles said. "I imagine both Mr. Henry and his assistant will be busy running the show this evening. Instead..." He looked around. The room swam with ladies and gentlemen in their finest gowns and suits, ready for an evening of entertainment. "There, let's go speak with the host."

The host, it seemed, knew precisely who we were asking about. "Oh, yes, he will be here," he said with a fervent nod. "You should be able to find him in Box A, through those doors."

"A box seat," Miles said. "That makes a great deal of sense."

"A private place to observe the actors," I said.

We made our way through the side door and up a short set of three stairs before turning the sharp corner of a narrow hall. The three doors along it stood open, light spilling out into the dim hall, and brass placards had been affixed to the wall beside each. We found the letter *A* outside the first door.

Miles peered in and gave me a nod before stepping inside. "Mr. Beecham?"

"Uh, yes?" answered a gruff, thick sort of voice. "Who is it?"

"I do apologize for bothering you sir, but my lady was hoping to meet you," he said, inclining his head.

"Oh, well, I would be very happy to meet an admirer," he said with a chuckle. "Do bring her in."

I stepped into the light, the beauty of the stage backdropping the box. Mr. Beecham was a much older man than I had initially imagined, but he must have been the sort who had been working in the business for many years. He seemed kindly enough, with wrinkles around his eyes from years of smiling, and thinning grey hair that he kept tied back behind his head. His nose hooked slightly at the end, and he squinted at me as I walked over to him.

"Ah, and what a lovely lady she is," he said, chortling again. He got to his feet, though somewhat unsteadily. He held out his hand as he grinned up at me, standing almost a head shorter than me. "What a pleasure it is to meet you. My name, as you already appear to know, is Beecham."

"And I am Miss Shipman," I said, shaking his hand.

"Shipman," he said, squinting further. "What a coincidence. I have recently met a Shipman, though she was not nearly as beautiful as you."

My face might have flushed if I had not nearly swallowed my tongue out of surprise. He mentioned Joan already! "Did you by any chance meet a Joan Shipman?" I asked.

"Yes, yes, I certainly did," he said. "Here, come, sit

with me and have a drink. We can discuss all these things. I would even be happy to give you an autograph...or perhaps an interview, eh?"

I looked over at Miles, and he gave me a curt nod. If I was going to get the answers I wanted, it was likely best to play the long game and get him to talk to me over the course of our conversation. I could not afford to become as angry with him as I had been with Mr. Baldwin, as I had great suspicion that it would not end well once again. I needed to maintain composure, and do it to the best of my ability.

"Thank you, sir, I would be happy to join you," I said.

He gestured to the seat beside him, which surveyed the whole of the theater below us; the lights still burned brightly overhead, and the hum of the theater goers echoed softly around the large room with its domed ceiling.

"Well, now, what brings you to me this evening, hmm?" he asked, reaching for a carafe filled with amber liquid. "Don't worry, my dear, I only have a liking for apple cider from Upstate. I do not partake in anything stronger. Perhaps you will join me in a glass?"

"Oh, well...thank you," I said, and took the proffered glass. I hoped he would not find my gloved hands strange, covering my aching, bruised hand and wrist.

"Are you here because you are looking for fame, or fortune? And you heard that Mr. Beecham is the one who can bring it to you?" He laughed again. "Ah, yes... it pleases me that my reputation precedes me."

"Sir, I was hoping that you could help me," I said, the cold of the cider making the tips of my fingers numb. "You see, I am looking for – "

"The next star?" he asked with a laugh. "Ah, yes... I am, too. And you hope that *you*, in fact, might be she? Well, I can tell you right now, you certainly have the face for theater. You would hardly need rouge with those rosy cheeks, and costuming would surely be easy with your lean frame and height."

"Well, thank you sir, but that is not what I am hoping for," I said. "My sister, you see, she – "

His eyes widened as he drew his glass to his lips, and gaped at me. "My word, how did I not see it before? Miss Joan, she is your *sister*, is she not?"

"Yes, sir, she is," I said, leaning forward in my seat, the cider forgotten. "I – "

"I should have seen the resemblance sooner," he said, beaming at me, shaking his head. "You have the same color eyes, and the same long neck. Yes, I found her quite becoming, just as yourself."

"Thank you, that is all very kind," I said. "But I must inform you that she has gone missing."

His smile faltered, and he became quickly sober. "Oh...well, I am sorry to hear that."

Relieved that he had finally ceased his barrage of nonsense, I took advantage of his newfound quiet. "Sir, it has come to my attention that she had recently met with you," I said. "She never told anyone in our family about the meeting, but I heard from a friend that she had sat down with you. Is this true?"

"Yes, it certainly is," he said. "But that was...well, almost a week ago now."

That means she met with him before I returned home from Newport, I thought. "What I want to know is what happened during your meeting," I said. "Did you happen to find her a job? Has she lined up a new performance somewhere that she has simply not told us of?"

"Well...I am sorry to tell you this, but your sister... she is not the star I have been looking for," he said. "I wish that was not the case, but I found her terribly uninteresting as a performer. I had asked her to memorize a monologue to perform for me, and when she did so, she seemed so...lifeless. It surprised me, I assure you, given her bright personality, but she simply was not what I have been looking for."

He found her uninteresting? I thought. How could he possibly have thought that about her? "All I want to know is if she said anything that might have indicated where we could find her," I said, trying to keep my emotions beneath the surface. "Her dream has been to be a serious actress, and if she has taken off somewhere in search of that – "

"I can assure you that I gave her no such direction," he said. "I politely informed her that I would be in touch, and to be honest, I have simply been far too busy to do so. I certainly hope you are able to find her, but I am afraid I have had nothing to do with it. Now...if *you* wanted to take the stage, I am certain I could find a beginner's role for you. I do not believe I would have you memorize a monologue like your sister. No, I should have you read me a sonnet, blindly, and – "

I glanced over the top of Mr. Beecham's head in Miles' direction. He wore a subtly irritated expression as well, arms crossed and eyeing the back of the old man's head. Mr. Beecham prattled on while I was trying to figure out how to proceed. Once again, we managed to find ourselves at a dead end of the investigation.

"Or..." Mr. Beecham said, stopping his long stream of thought. He spun around in his seat and pointed at Miles. "This young man. *He* is made for the stage. His face has a very distinctive look –"

"I am terribly sorry, sir, but my focus is my work for the Shipman family," Miles said, a bit curtly as he bowed his head.

"That is a shame, really, as you would quickly become a favorite," Mr. Beecham said. "I can assure you that the opportunities I could send your way – "

"Once again, sir, thank you for the compliment, but I simply cannot abandon my employers," he said.

Mr. Beecham shrugged his shoulders. "Very well," he said.

I set the cider down on the low wall around the box seats. My shoulder throbbed; I could feel my very heartbeat in the muscles that were attempting to heal. "Mr. Beecham, I appreciate your time, I realize that you are a terribly busy man. I thank you for being willing to talk with me about my sister...but as you can imagine, we have a great deal that we are trying to do in order to find her."

"Yes, yes, of course, of course," he said with a wave and a smile. "If you do find her, please inform her that I shall not be taking her on as a client. I fear she lacks the spark I am looking for."

I had risen from my seat, and stiffened as I turned to leave. I had thought he at least *seemed* sympathetic. In truth, he was no better than many of those in the acting business that I had been acquainted with. Shallow, selfish, and deceptive.

My anger, ever simmering beneath the surface, spiked. "You, sir, are missing an opportunity of a lifetime by turning her down," I snapped, glaring down at him, hardly caring that anyone in the nearby seats or neighboring boxes could hear me. "Joan has talent. But more importantly than that, you cared so little for my family, for the suffering we are going through – and then, to turn around and try to buy me off in the next breath – and my butler too!"

He held up his hands, the smile entirely faded from his face. "I – I am sorry," he sputtered. "Please know I have no idea what happened to your sister! I cannot afford to get caught up with the police!"

"I have never accused you – " I began.

"I had nothing to do with it!" he interrupted. "Get out! Now!"

Miles reached out and took hold of my arm, helping me along the row and up the stairs back to the narrow hall.

"Sylvia – " he said as we reached the foyer.

"No," I said, my eyes stinging. "No, I do not want to talk about it..."

I stormed off toward the door, ignoring the glances of the last stragglers into the theater, and the shuddering and searing pain all this motion had awoken in my muscles.

I hurried down the stairs, and slipped on the very last step. I started to feel myself going, but an arm caught me around the waist.

I did not even have to turn around to know it was Miles.

"Sylvia..." he said gently.

I shook my head, the cold stinging my face and eyes even as hot tears splashed down onto my cheeks.

"I am – I am farther from Joan than I have been yet," I said, suddenly weary, burying my head in my hands. "I – I am so frightened..."

He turned me around to hold me against him, drawing me away toward the wall. I relinquished my better judgment and laid my head against his shoulder. I cried and I cried, the emotions rolling one after the other.

"I...just need to go back to the house," I said.

"Are you sure?" he asked, his breath tickling my ear.

"Yes," I said, stepping away from him to put a little distance between us. I needed to focus. I needed to regain control of myself. "I need – I need to find out what my parents have learned."

"All right," he said. "Then let's head back."

He helped me into the car, saying nothing as we started off once again.

Had it been worth it to try and stand up for Joan? Had it been worth it to let that talent scout know exactly what I thought of him?

No, of course not.

Maybe I should not have been the one to do this. Maybe Father had been right to hire a private investigator. I was too deeply involved. I could not detach myself enough to consider the case clearly. Would I be able to find her? Could I manage to keep calm enough to be able to investigate?

It made little sense, all of it. All of our sources had gone dry. I was no closer to finding Joan than I had been when we first found out she had gone missing.

"I was hoping that man could provide answers for us..." I murmured when we were halfway home.

"I know," Miles said.

I crossed my arms. "When I find Joan, I need to convince her to leave this whole theater dream of hers behind. The people she interacts with do not deserve her attention."

"Perhaps they do not," Miles agreed. "Perhaps after all of this, she will lose interest in the whole business, but that's a decision only she can make."

My cheeks burned. It was one matter for me to speak of Joan as if she were alive and well...but when Miles did, it felt as if he were dishonoring her in some way.

If she is dead...then none of this matters anyway. Should I have been looking sooner? Should I have stayed up all through the night last night? Was I too slow somehow? Too late?

No. I could not operate that way. I had allowed the despair of the situation to infiltrate my heart and mind too much already. I needed to act as if she were alive and well if I truly planned to finish this case.

"Regardless...I hope Mother and Father found out something," I said. "Or maybe she has even returned home during our time away."

"Maybe she has, Miss Sylvia..." Miles said.

I did not take kindly to the hollow disbelief in his voice, but chose to dismiss it all the same.

10

L onging ached within me, as if the sheer depth of my hope could will Joan into reality. I hoped beyond all sensible reason that when Miles and I arrived back home she would be there, waiting for me, prepared to chide me for allowing my fears to get the better of me.

If I knew she was dead beyond a shadow of a doubt, at least I could mourn her properly, I thought dismally. *This uncertainty is surely going to drive me to the edge of madness...if not outright over the cliff.*

My mother's voice bounced down the hall the moment we stepped into the house. Miles gave me a wary glance as he helped me with my cloak. Her laughter grated against my already raw nerves, and part of me wanted nothing more than to turn around and hurry back out the door. I had been so certain that I could face my parents...but hearing my mother now made me frustrated and irritated.

I found the pair of them in the dining room, finishing up what seemed to be an incredibly late dinner. Mother lounged comfortably in her chair. Father sat at the head of the table halfway through a lemon ice, which seemed a surprisingly decadent treat in the middle of winter when lemons were so expensive to come by...especially this year.

I hoped more than anything that they would not be able to see the bruising on my forehead, or any bulking around my shoulder from the bandages.

"Look who decided to finally join us," Father said, lifting his eyes to me as I walked into the room.

"Oh, Sylvie, dear, *there* you are," Mother crooned. "You should thank Mrs. Riley, who insisted that we wait up for you, though I am surprised you are home already. Were you not attending a play this evening?"

"Yes, I did," I said. "I decided that I did not want to stay."

"Why ever not?" Mother asked, her brow furrowing.

"It is difficult to imagine sitting through a play when it is something that Joan liked to do so much," I said.

Mother frowned, reaching over to lay her hand on

my arm. "Missing her, hmm? Well, do not worry too much, dear. I am certain that the private investigator your father hired will find her."

My heart stirred, and I chanced a look at my father. The movement made my shoulder twinge, and I did my best to keep my face blank. I did not need to have him detect my pain and make me explain about the accident. "Have you heard anything, by any chance?"

Father shook his head as he took another spoonful of his lemon ice. "I could hardly expect to, given the fact that he just left for California. It could be many days before he makes progress."

I blanched, my eyes widening. "*Many days?*" I breathed. "What if something happens to her during that time?"

"Such as what?" Mother asked.

I looked at her, and my heart ached at the innocent expression on her face. She truly could not imagine something horrific happening to her daughter, or her fears simply would not allow her to do so. Her refusal to admit that something might have gone wrong infuriated me...but could I blame her for being so frightened that she allowed herself to live blissfully ignorant?

Yes...yes, I can, because she is her mother – my mother – and she is allowing her feelings to get in the way of common sense, or from the reality of what we could really be doing to help Joan.

"Father, are you quite certain that was the right thing to do?" I asked. "Can we be certain this man will be able to help?"

"He is one of the best in the city at what he does," Father said with a dismissive wave. "Personally recommended to me by one of my clients."

*Who have always proven to be reliable...*I thought sarcastically. "While I am pleased that he is well-known, what is his success rate?"

Father said nothing, simply staring at me.

"Has he solved many cases?" I asked again.

"Well, I never asked him that," he said, averting his gaze back to his lemon ice. "As he comes so highly recommended, he has surely earned that reputation by being successful."

"One can certainly hope..." I murmured.

I glanced over my good shoulder, spotting Miles standing along the wall. He watched my father cautiously, his own expression saddened. He must have felt my eyes, for he turned to look at me in question. I could nearly hear the question he was thinking.

Are you going to tell them?

I had debated it the whole way home. My investigation had led me down many paths already, but none of them had proved successful. How could I possibly sit there and tell them that I had been searching all over the city, yet had nothing to show for it? Not only would it disappoint them, but it might further encourage them in the idea that Joan had indeed fled to California.

*Perhaps it is time that I considered they could be right...*I thought.

Yet, as much as I would have liked to believe it, I could not get past some glaring flaws in the notion, the greatest of which was her meeting with the talent scout. According to him, he had not had the chance to inform her that he had chosen not to take her on as a client. She didn't know. So, why would she go to California if there was a chance she could still make something of herself in her home city? It made no sense.

I shook my head for Miles to see, and he nodded, settling himself back against the wall.

I intended to tell them, but I wanted answers first. I could not come to them empty-handed. If I was going to give them closure, one way or the other, then I needed to keep investigating.

How, though...that was another matter entirely.

"I'm sorry, but I am going to retire for the evening..." I said. At once, Miles was behind my chair, ready to pull it out for me. "If you will excuse me."

"Oh, come now, dear, please stay and have your dessert with us," Mother said. "Surely you need not go to bed so soon."

"I am not feeling terribly well," I said.

Father said nothing as I stepped away from the table, simply watching me as I made my way to the door.

"Well...take care, dear," Mother said. "I will send Mrs. Riley up with peppermint tea for you. Do you want honey?"

"That's fine, Mother," I said, and walked out.

Miles followed me. "Is everything all right?" he asked.

"I need to be alone for a little while," I said, and started up the stairs. I could feel his gaze on me as I made my way up, but refused to look back at him. I did not have the strength to discuss the matter right now, even if there had not been a horrendous pain in my left half, and a dull throbbing in my skull.

I knotted my fingers in my hair as I blindly made my way down the hall, frustration and sorrow mingling like oil and water in my stomach.

I stopped outside Joan's door, and then some impulse tempted me to step inside.

Hopelessness enveloped me, as I plunged into the darkness of her room, giving myself over to the despair that had haunted me since she had disappeared.

I threw myself onto her bed, ignoring the protests of my aching body, sprawling out over the quilt that she had chosen from a quaint little shop near our summer home two years before. She had loved the design in the corners of the birds in flight. Would she ever see it again? Would I ever be able to look at it without sadness?

I lay there, lost in worry for what might have been minutes, or it might have been hours. It mattered little, as I would have felt the same regardless.

I rolled onto my back, staring up at the canopy of her bed, draped in emerald curtains. She had loved velvet –

Why must I be so utterly convinced that she is gone? Why is it that I cannot imagine her still living?

I knew why. My recent experiences with murders and deaths...all of them were playing in to the already frightened and negative feelings I had about the situation. They had caused my senses to be heightened, overly paranoid, seeing threats in every shadow...

I drew in a deep breath, knowing loss of control was nothing more than momentary catharsis. It would not bring Joan back, and it would not help me to find what happened to her.

My fist slammed against the mattress, anger pulsing through me at my own foolishness. How could I allow myself to give up so easily?

A creak at the door made me sit up, and Miles stepped into the room.

"I said that I wanted to be alone," I reminded him.

"Forgive me for choosing to ignore your wishes..."

he said. "Especially when you are as troubled as you are."

I said nothing as he closed the door behind himself and strode over to a lamp near the bed. There was a clicking sound and, a moment later, the bulb flared to life, casting a pool of warm light across the floor and bedspread.

He grabbed the chair at Joan's desk and dragged it over the rug to set it down in front of me. Without a word, he sat both it and himself down.

"I do not know what you want me to say..." I said, my throat tight.

Miles studied me, his eyes narrowing. "Can I get you anything?" he asked.

"Answers, for one," I said.

"You know that if I could, I would not hesitate – "

"I know..." I said, laughing hollowly. "I know."

"I do still believe we can find her," Miles said. "It has not been too long."

"Are you quite sure?" I asked. "Any moment that passes could make it too long."

"That is true," he said. "However, I was thinking of this. It is incredibly rare that someone would have... say, *kidnapped* Joan without reason, yes? As such, that reason would likely come to light."

"How do you mean?" I asked.

"Ransom money," he said. "Joan cannot very well give a kidnapper any such thing, yes? Your father is the one with the wealth readily available, and that means that it is likely only a matter of time until he would hear from someone demanding money."

I straightened. "I had not considered that. It is a good point. It means that if there is a kidnapper and they want something, then they will need Joan alive."

"Precisely," Miles said.

I clapped my hands together, hope surging through me like a strike of hot lightning, igniting my soul once again. I hopped up, my nerves humming with excitement. "Miles, you are a genius," I said. "If they need her, she is likely safe for the moment!"

He nodded. "That is precisely my thinking as well."

"Oh, why did I not think of this before?" I breathed, my mind racing faster than I could keep up with. "This means we have more time."

"We very likely do, yes," he said.

"Where do we go now, though?" I asked. "We have no leads."

"I would not say we do not have any..." Miles said. "I still believe that we have Mr. Baldwin."

My eyes narrowed. "That monster is not going to talk to us," I said.

"No, he likely will not," Miles said. "But think for a moment, Miss Sylvia. Set your emotions aside. You must! I realize this whole situation is upsetting to you, but you cannot allow your frustration to keep rearing its head."

I frowned. "You are speaking quite boldly, Miles."

"Yes, I am," he said, also getting to his feet, his gaze sharp. "I am doing so because you *need* to hear this."

I swallowed. Perhaps I did. "How are we going to get the truth out of him?"

"Think about it," he said. "If Mr. Baldwin will not work with us, then who will?"

I folded my arms. "I suppose – I don't know, a friend?"

"Anyone else?"

"A family member?" I asked. "Someone who would be willing to betray him?"

"Go on..." Miles said, twirling his finger in the air as if reeling in a fish on a lure.

My eyes widened. "What about a member of his household staff?"

Miles snapped his fingers. "There we are!" he said.

"If he even has any of those..." I said.

"He mentioned his servant who failed to answer the door, so there is at least one person to tend to his house," Miles said. "And there are probably more. Though he lives in a less than desirable neighborhood, I cannot imagine someone who considers himself so high and mighty would not have some form of staff."

"With what money, though?" I asked.

"Well, did you not say that he hoped to marry well?" Miles asked. "Sought out only the wealthiest of women to spend his time with?"

"Yes," I said.

"Then he could not very well live in complete squalor," Miles said. "I imagine he keeps a skeleton crew, just enough to maintain a house while he is out frolicking around and trying to impress wealthy friends."

"I suppose it is worth the look..." I said, then my brow furrowed. "But what about his family? Or friends?"

Miles shook his head. "Servants have a higher chance of not holding absolute loyalty toward the families they work for, unless they have earned it," he said. "You understand this, I'm sure. If your father treated all the members of his staff badly, they would be rather easy to coerce and bribe."

"My father is good to his staff," I said, somewhat defensively.

Miles nodded. "I would very much agree," he said. "Do not think that to be a criticism, for I greatly admire his behavior in that regard. He has changed my mind on many things that I might not have done so well myself in the past..." His gaze became distant for a moment, and then he shook it off. "All I am saying is that a man like Baldwin may not be so generous to his people. Therefore, he will likely have no love from them."

"Which means that it might be easy to get them to tell us about him," I said. My eyes widened. "Perhaps they will remember my sister. Maybe they have seen her there." Then my skin went icy cold. "Oh, I certainly hope they would not have seen her there, perhaps maybe heard about her – "

"Do not allow yourself to get lost in your fears, Miss Sylvia," Miles said. "What do you say? Should we go to speak with his household staff?"

"Yes," I said, but my eyes drifted toward the small, gold-faced clock on Joan's end table. It was almost nine o'clock. "Though the hour is likely too late to go and speak with them now."

"I say we try all the same," Miles said. "He may very well be out for the evening."

My heart stirred. "And I suppose if he is home then we can simply return in the morning."

"Yes," Miles said.

"And during that time, if someone has taken her, they may well send a ransom note to my father," I said. "Which I could then use to try and find her before he has to hand over any amount of money."

"Right," Miles said. "I truly do believe we still have the upper hand."

"Then let us not waste any more time," I said. "We should head straight to Baldwin's home and hope those there will be willing to help us."

Miles grinned. "It does me good to see life in your eyes again, Miss Sylvia."

Despite the fear gnawing at my insides, I returned

the smile. "Well...I can either sit here and wallow, or I can do something. And for the sake of my sister, I choose to do something."

"Very good," Miles said, striding to the door, throwing it open. "Then let us be on our way."

11

___

"Perhaps you are right, Miles," I said as he drove us down the street where Mr. Baldwin resided. "These houses are not quite as terrible as I remember from earlier."

"They are old," Miles said. "In need of some repair, but I imagine these are the sort of homes that once were magnificent. As with all places, rot and decay crept in and changed the neighborhood for the worse."

I looked around, and saw the age in the cracked bricks, in the inconsistently lit street lamps, in the woman in the worn dress sweeping the front steps with a glare as we passed by. *Rot and decay crept in...* If only that were not the truth.

Miles pulled up alongside the sidewalk, a few houses down from Mr. Baldwin's. "We should walk, and perhaps go around to the back," he said. "We have no need to see Baldwin."

"Right," I said. "Do you suppose they will answer if we go there?"

"Certainly," Miles said. "Mrs. Riley and I greet deliverymen and other visitors for the staff via the back door of the kitchen quite often."

I nodded. "Very well," I said. "Then let us try."

"The hour may be a bit unconventional, but it would not be the first time that I have encountered someone visiting after hours," he said. "Come on, then."

We started down the sidewalk, the sounds of the city pressing in around us; car horns honking, dogs barking, streetlights humming. I gripped my purse firmly and reached out to slide my arm beneath Miles'. He smoothly moved so as to draw me nearer to him. *Best to stay close to him at this time of night,* I thought. *I would rather people assume we were together instead of thinking me alone and easy to rob.*

We took the first turn down the narrow alley between two of the rowhouses, making our way to the roadway behind them. A single streetlight glowed dimly, barely enough to light the way. Miles slowed his gait.

"What number was his house, again?" he asked in a low murmur, a puff of warm air hovering in front of his nose.

"I don't quite recall…" I said. "Wait, was it not the second to the last from the end of the row?"

"Yes, I think you are right," he said.

It turned out that we were wrong. The kitchen cook that belonged to the second to last house chose some colorful words to tell us off with, before Miles managed to obtain the real location of Mr. Baldwin's home. It happened to be two doors further down.

"I certainly hope whoever lives with Mr. Baldwin has better manners," I said, smoothing some of the dirt from the front of my cloak.

We made our way down to the proper door, and I held my breath as Miles knocked.

The door was answered faster than I expected. A balding man with a large nose and thick eyebrows appeared, his eyes narrowing as they fell upon us. "Do you have any idea what time it is?"

"We certainly do," Miles said. "Is this the home of Mr. Baldwin?"

"It is," said the man, seeming reluctant as he remained only visible behind a crack in the open door-way. "But Mr. Baldwin is not expecting visitors so late – "

"We are not friends of Mr. Baldwin," I cut in, unable to stop myself. "The very furthest from it, in fact."

"My apologies, sir, my name is Miles, and I am the butler for the Shipman family – "

"I do not much care who you are," the man said, though his expression had changed to one more of worry than of anger. "What I do care about is why you are here at such a late hour?"

"Is your master home?" Miles asked.

"No," the man said.

"Then may we ask you some questions about him?" Miles asked.

"Once again, I should like to know why you are here," the man answered crossly. "I will hear that before I am willing to share any further information with you."

My hand squeezed the inside of Miles' arm, and he hesitated before speaking. He glanced down at me, and then nodded to me.

"My name is Miss Sylvia Shipman, and I am looking into my sister's disappearance," I said. "I was recently informed that she and your master were acquainted, and perhaps involved with one another romantically. He refused to speak with us when we attempted to, and I am convinced that he knows more than he has been letting on."

The man's face became as blank as a fresh sheet of paper. "You say that you are looking for your sister?" he asked. He glanced over his shoulder, as if considering something.

My heart swelled within me. I hoped that he would help, that he understood my plight.

The man sighed, shaking his head. He pulled the door open wider. "Come inside. But be quiet."

Miles took my hand and swept me in through the door before the man closed it behind us. We had stepped into a small kitchen with a low ceiling, from which a handsome set of cast iron pots hung above a stove. A long, worn table stretched across the narrow space, littered with ceramic bowls, wooden plates, and silver utensils, many of which were mismatched.

"Make yourselves comfortable," he said, gesturing to a pair of stools around the table, likely used to prep for the meals. He strode toward the stove, where there was a steaming tea kettle. "I was just making tea. Would either of you care for some?"

"Thank you, that is very kind," Miles said. "And is there a name by which we can call you?"

"My name is Daniel, though I suppose many call me Mr. Baldwin," he said, finding a trio of tea cups, one of which seemed to be chipped along the bottom.

My head snapped toward Miles. Mr. Baldwin? But that would mean –

"And no, I am not *your* Mr. Baldwin's father," he said, lifting the kettle off the stovetop, carrying it back to the table. "I am his uncle."

"His uncle?" I repeated. "Yet you are employed by him?"

"Unless you are simply here watching his house for him?" Miles asked.

Daniel shook his head, sighing. "No...I am working for him, unfortunately. And if you have met my nephew, then you know full well what a joy that is."

This may be exactly what we are looking for, I thought. "How did you come to work for your own nephew?" I asked.

"I owed a great deal of debt to his father," Daniel said. "Most of which has been repaid, but he refuses to let me leave yet, continually inventing excuses and reasons why I still owe him."

"How cruel," I said.

He pursed his lips as he poured the water into the cups, and then reached for a tin canister filled with loose tea leaves.

"I assume that you know something about Miss Sylvia's family," Miles said, crossing his arms. "Given the fact that you let us in. Or at the very least, you recognized her name."

"That I did..." Daniel said rather heavily. "The Shipman name has been repeated frequently as of late in this house..."

"How so?" Miles asked.

Daniel poured the tea leaves into a pewter tea ball before settling it into the nearest cup. "I'm sorry, but I do not think it would be wise for me to repeat what I know – "

"Daniel, please..." I said. "I don't know if my sister

is alive or dead. If you are aware of anything that could help us, then I would be forever in your debt."

Daniel said nothing as he reached for a small jar of honey, spooning some into the tea. "This could land me in a great deal of trouble if he ever finds out," he said, glancing toward the door opposite us, closed tight. "Even put me in danger."

"I understand..." I said. "But a young woman's life could be at stake."

He scooped the tea ball out, emptied it, and filled it again before dipping it into the next teacup. I hesitated to question him, for I knew that pushing him could end up backfiring. I needed to be patient, try to wait him out.

He glanced up at me in the dim light of the room. "Would you care for any honey?" he asked. "Or do you take it black?"

"I would be happy to have some honey," I said.

He nodded, passing the finished tea cup to me. It had been painted with delicate tiger lilies, trimmed with gold leaf. The warmth bled into my fingers, yet it did not reach my soul or soothe my fears. I could not look away from Daniel. I feared that his response would not end up being what I wanted to hear.

He cleared his throat, bouncing the tea ball in the second cup. "I am sorry to tell you, Miss Sylvia...but I do not know where your sister is."

I licked my lips, my heart plummeting. Why had I

allowed myself to hope that he would be the answer to all my prayers? That had been foolish of me...

"I suppose that might have been too much to ask," I said, setting the teacup down. The very smell of the honey turned my stomach now.

"That doesn't mean that I have not heard...something that might be of use."

I froze, and the room fell silent for a few moments.

"What do you know?" I asked.

He passed the second cup to Miles. "Honey?" he asked.

"No, thank you," Miles said. "What is it that you know, Daniel?"

He dropped his voice, leaning forward over the third teacup he was preparing. "I have overheard a number of discussions that my nephew has had in the past few weeks with another person. A woman, though I do not know who she is. I never had the chance to see her face. As you can imagine, I did not want to let it be known that I was listening in on his conversations..."

"What was said in these discussions?" I asked.

"I might not have paid any attention to his conversations, as they typically never hold much substance. However, I managed to catch him say the word *steal,* and immediately it made me pause outside the door to listen."

"Steal?" Miles asked. "Steal what?"

"That conversation was quite elusive, apart from

the fact that they were certain all their preparations were going to be worthwhile, that they had been able to get away with it up to that point. The young woman said something about no one else being wise to their plans, and they laughed. I remember distinctly my nephew mocking the person they had been trying to fool for believing them in the first place."

"I still don't understand what this has to do with me, or my sister," I said, my forehead wrinkling, my brows drawing together.

"The next evening, that woman returned. I knew I had to listen in on their discussion. When I did, I heard them mention the name of the house they were planning to rob...which happened to be the Shipman residence."

My stomach dropped to the floor. "What in the world could they be after?" I asked. I looked over at Miles.

"Did they mention what they were after?" Miles asked.

Daniel shook his head, spooning some honey into his own tea before giving it a gentle swirl. "Unfortunately, I never heard what it was they were hoping to take. All I can assume is that it was something precious. Something valuable."

I chewed on the inside of my lip. Something did seem incredibly strange, did it not? I looked at Miles again, the movement sending a sharp throb through my head at the spot where it had struck the window earlier. "I cannot think of what single item they could want," I said. "I suppose if they were after my mother's ring collection, or perhaps my father's library... But how could they possibly hope to make off with that?"

"I don't know," Daniel said. "I imagine it would have to be one particular piece, the way they were discussing it."

I looked at Miles again. "Is there anything you can think of that they might have been after? Has my father recently acquired something of great worth?"

Miles frowned, shaking his head. His eyes swept over the surface of the table as if he could see every inch of our house there. "No," he said. "In fact, he has gone to great lengths to get rid of a great deal, as you know."

I folded my arms, careful with my aching shoulder. "I suppose we have a rather expansive collection of heirlooms from both sides of my family," I said. I huffed. "I have no idea what item it could have been, though."

"I imagine it would be something they could carry out of the house," Daniel said.

"Maybe even something small enough that it could be pocketed," I agreed, a twist knotting my stomach. "Oh, dear... What if they wanted my grandmother's ring? Or perhaps my grandfather's cigar case?"

Miles shook his head. "I realize why you would find

those valuable, but for a thief, they would be looking for something made of precious metal, or gemstones. Something a broker would be able to resell. Artwork, a rare piece of furniture, perhaps even an article of clothing."

"But what?" I said. "I can think of nothing we have that would tempt anyone."

"I don't know..." Miles said. "Neither can I."

"Is it possible there are any other Shipman homes in the city?" Daniel asked.

"Well... I do have family," I said. "But what makes you say this has any connection to Joan?"

"Because they mentioned her name specifically," Daniel said.

I sighed. "All right, then there is no doubt it is our home," I said. Then it struck me. "You don't suppose the only reason why Mr. Baldwin has given her any attention is because he learned of this valuable item and hoped to befriend her to get closer to it?"

"That is a good question," Miles said. "And it would explain his indifferent behavior when we spoke with him compared to what other people had seen previously."

"Right," I said. "The theater director said that he had been excessive with his affections toward her, and Father was so utterly convinced he was trying to pursue her that he told her off."

"Did Baldwin have any real affection for Miss Joan?" Miles asked Daniel.

"That I do not know," he said. "He never spoke of her to me."

Everything was beginning to make more and more sense. "Then his interest in her only had to do with whatever it is they were going to steal – " I looked up at Daniel. "Have they said when they planned to go after the object?"

He shook his head. "No, I can only assume it was soon because of how often the young woman was around here talking about it."

"I would like to know who this young woman was," I said. "Having more than one suspect to talk with would be useful."

"There is one more thing you should know," Daniel said. "They mentioned a place, just last night."

"Last night?" I asked.

"What place?" Miles asked.

"He mentioned the southside docks," Daniel said. "Said they had left something there that they needed to go and check on."

My hand snapped over to Miles', grasping his wrist. Pain shot through my arm, my hand stinging beneath the bandages. I ignored it. "Miles, that must be where they're keeping Joan!"

"Is that not where there are an abundance of abandoned buildings?" Miles asked.

"Yes," Daniel said, his eyes widening. "Oh, my word... When they said they had left something, I assumed they meant the object they were going to steal."

My heart thundered in my chest. "No, they couldn't have," I said. "We were just at home, and have been for much of the day. If anything had been already taken, we would have learned about it."

"Which means the object they left can only be one thing – " Miles said.

"That *must* be where Joan is!" I exclaimed. "And Miles, you were right. They may not be keeping her for a ransom, but they need her to help them locate the item they're after."

"That's true," Miles said. "But that means they may only want her around until they manage to steal it."

"Which could very well be tonight..." I said, a shiver running through me. "Mr. Baldwin is out, and we aren't back at the house."

"We need to go and find Joan," Miles said. "As soon as possible."

"Right," I said. "Daniel, did they happen to say which building they were keeping her in?"

"No, but the girl did mention the steep staircase they had to take, along with the smell of fish across the street," he said.

"Which means it is likely right near the fish canning factory down there," Miles said.

I clapped my hands together. "We have no time to waste! We have to get to her!"

"All right," Miles said. "Are you all right, though, Miss Sylvia?"

"Why do you ask?" I asked.

"The bruising on your forehead..." Miles said, his eyes drifting to my forehead. "It seems to have spread."

I reached up and gingerly touched my forehead.

"Here," Daniel said, turning around and reaching for a cobalt blue glass bottle. "I can give you some tonic to help if you have an injury."

"No, I'm fine," I said. "In fact, I feel better than I have since this all began. We are this close to finding Joan, and I am certain there is nothing that can take that away from me. Not even some aches and pains."

Miles grinned. "Do not push yourself," he said. "Well, thank you, Daniel. We appreciate your help, truly. I can assure you that we will not tell anyone you helped us unless you would be willing to share with the police when your nephew is inevitably arrested."

"I would be glad to testify if it comes down to it," he said. "But also... I hoped that I might come along with the two of you."

I glanced at him. "Why?" I asked.

"I might be able to talk my nephew down if something happens," he said.

I looked over at Miles. "What do you think?"

"The more there are of us, the easier we will be to

detect," he said. "But he does know his nephew better than we do. His understanding might prove useful."

"I say we bring him," I said. "Maybe Mr. Baldwin will think twice about doing anything if he knows that his family has become aware of his plans."

Daniel nodded, squaring his shoulders.

"Then let us be on our way," Miles said. "It will take us a half hour to reach the southside docks."

My stomach twisted. "We can only hope the thieves don't reach my house in the time it takes us to find Joan."

12

The southside docks were a bit of folklore to the children of the city. Like many fairy tales, they were told as a means of deterring us from bad behavior. The docks were either haunted or filled with corpses, depending on the severity of the punishment. The one difference between the stories of the docks and any other tales we read about in books... was that the adults were often as frightened as the children.

As such, there was hardly a soul I knew that would willingly go down to that part of the city. Dangerous people were said to linger there. Nowadays, I could only imagine that the abandoned buildings and factories had grown more dilapidated than when I was a child. And given the hour...

"I do worry about bringing a lady with us to this

part of town," Daniel said, gazing out through the windows.

"In my experience, Miss Sylvia is well able to handle herself," Miles reassured him. "Now, you said that you overheard Mr. Baldwin's companion describing the stairs...and the terrible fish smell." He slowed the car, and pointed out through the front windshield. "Is that perhaps the source of the smell?"

The fish cannery sat on the corner overlooking the bay. I glanced across the street. Three warehouses stood in a row, all of them appearing entirely unused. "Do you suppose she is over here?"

"I think it likely," Daniel answered uncertainly.

"One thing I wonder," Miles said. "Why did Baldwin come all the way here to hide Joan?"

"I imagine it was because his father's business used to be in one of the warehouses," Daniel said. "Until a few years ago when he could no longer make the rent payments for the space. He went bankrupt, and there was nothing he could do but abandon a great deal of the stock. As it happens, no one picked up the space, and so, it has sat empty like a great deal of these buildings around."

"So he's familiar with the area, and has no doubt selected a place he would have known, but no one else would have," I said. I shook my head. "I am glad we crossed paths with you, Daniel."

He nodded. "It is good, indeed. I only hope we are able to settle this without all sorts of trouble."

"As do I," Miles said. "Though given your nephew's behavior, I cannot imagine he will be terribly happy that we have interfered with his plans."

"Perhaps we should have gone to the police before coming here..." I said.

"I think we might have put Joan's life in greater danger had we done that," Miles said.

"He is right," Daniel said. "I fear that if my nephew feels trapped he may resort to drastic action."

"Very well," I said. "Then I suppose we can only hope to rescue her while he is away and return back to my family's house before he and his accomplice manage to sneak in and steal whatever it is they are after."

Miles pulled the car up beside the canning factory, careful to keep the lights pointed away from the nearest abandoned warehouse. We did not want to give Mr. Baldwin any indication of our location. The three of us exited the car and hurried across the quiet street. A cat yowled somewhere nearby, sending my nerves singing.

The warehouse door stood isolated along the wall, with windows several stories above. Water damage had caused the east side of the wall to begin to crumble, chunks of the bricks peppering the sidewalk below.

"We should not use the main entrance..." Miles

said.

"I agree," Daniel said. "It might be being watched."

"Do you know your way around this place?" I asked.

"It has been years since I was here last," Daniel said. "But I think I should be able to navigate my way through."

"Very good," Miles said. "Then let us be on our way."

We made our way around the side of the building, finding a staff entrance sunken down in a basement. It did not surprise me all together to find it unlocked, given the sort of environment we were in. We slipped inside, and as the door closed behind us, we were enveloped in complete darkness.

The damp air hung heavily around us, smelling strongly of mildew and rot. I swallowed hard, trying not to panic as my eyes adjusted to the darkness.

"How are we supposed to find anything in here?" I murmured. Even my quiet whispers bounced off the cold, stone walls around us.

"Do not worry, Miss," Miles said, reaching into the front of his jacket. "I brought something in case we ran into a problem like this." He withdrew a small pewter lighter, and with a flick of his thumb, a flame sprung to life. "I cannot guarantee that it has enough fuel, but it will help get us out of the basement."

The golden light bounced off the damp walls all

around us, revealing a cylindrical tunnel that disappeared into the darkness further ahead.

*This place is enormous...*I lamented in the quiet of my heart. *How are we supposed to find Joan? It could take hours.*

"Where is your brother's old warehouse storage?" Miles whispered.

"On the third floor," Daniel said. "Though I must admit, coming in from down here has turned me around a bit."

"We will find our way," Miles said.

A scraping above us sent shivers down my spine, and I drew nearer to Miles.

At once, he snapped the top of the lighter closed, enveloping us in damp darkness once more.

In the silence we waited. I craned my ears, my eyes sweeping over the ceiling for more of the sound.

There must be people here, I thought. *Joan? Is that you?*

My heartbeats were like the fluttering of a bird's wings. She could truly be this close!

"Shall we go on?" Miles whispered.

"Yes," I replied.

The tiny flame reignited, and slowly Miles started down the hall. I went after, and Daniel followed along behind us.

The hall shared few secrets, with only a pair of doorways, both of which were locked. Daniel murmured that a set of stairs would likely be at the end of the corridor, and we simply needed to keep pressing forward.

Breathing became difficult, as each breath coated the inside of my mouth with what tasted like stagnant sea water. I tried to draw in slow, deep breaths, but the expansion of my chest only caused searing pain through my shoulder. My head throbbed, and I had to pinch my eyes closed to keep the room from spinning.

"It looks as if the corridor comes to a fork up ahead," Miles whispered, gesturing in front of himself. "Daniel, any recommendations?"

"I would imagine there might be a sign," Daniel answered, coming up to us.

He had good sense about him, as there was indeed a sign. "Look, stairs!" I said. "This way!" I started down the hall, into the darkness. I could not stand the tension of waiting to find Joan any longer. My eyes had adjusted just enough that I could make out the edges of the corridor, and with Miles' light behind me, it helped me to see at least my shadow along the length of the stone floor before it mingled with the darkness up ahead.

My heart skipped as the light illuminated what quickly became a stair, and then another, and soon a full staircase leading up. Excitement washed through me, and I hurried toward it.

Somewhere up above us, an enormous *BANG*

echoed through the hall, followed by a series of loud shouts.

I nearly lost my footing as an arm wrapped around my middle, drawing me back away from the stairs. I opened my mouth to shriek, but a hand clamped tightly over it.

Panic flooded my mind, causing it to go entirely blank, as hot breath brushed against my cheek.

"Quiet."

Sweet relief that I could almost taste filled me when I realized that it was only Miles. I nodded against his hand, and he relinquished his hold. I turned my eyes up the stairs even as Miles extinguished the flame once again.

The words were muffled through the floor, but it became quickly apparent there were three different voices, all male. Another *BANG* echoed down the stairs, and I winced at the sound as it sent tremors through my body.

It might have felt longer, but a few moments later the voices began to fade away. Miles let out a breath and flicked the light back on. "We need to be careful," he said. "It is possible we will have to cross their path in order to reach the next set of stairs."

"I don't know if that's true," Daniel said in a low murmur. "If I remember correctly, I believe this stair-case winds all the way up to the top floor."

"That would be good news..." Miles said. "I do not

much care to pass by a group of inebriated, homeless men in a setting like this."

"Nor I..." I said.

"Come on, then," Miles said. "Let's see what we can find."

We took great care climbing the stairs. I looked up, and managed to catch a glimpse of some light bleeding between the railings of the stairs several stories above us, trickling down to where we were almost all the way in the basement. Was it moonlight? Or light from the streetlamps outside?

I wondered if Joan was sitting in complete darkness? And if she was, for how long? "We need to hurry," I whispered, trying to take the stairs as quickly as I dared without making any unnecessary sound.

I reached the landing of the main floor just behind Miles, stepping into a large receiving room that had been almost entirely stripped bare. The immense rolling doors seemed to be the only distinctive feature, most of which were easy to see from the light filtering in from the high windows above our heads. Compared to the dank dark of the basement corridor, this might as well have been as bright as day.

"We should keep climbing," Miles said, pocketing the lighter. We would be able to make our way from here. "We don't want to meet those vagrants. I worry what they might do."

"Do you suppose Mr. Baldwin will have asked them

to watch the door for someone coming to look for Joan?" I murmured.

Miles pressed his finger to his lips, but nodded as he started up the next staircase. I glanced further into the enormous room, and thought I caught sight of fire-light somewhere in the depths of the cavernous space... I did not linger to inspect it further.

I slipped up after Miles, with Daniel close behind me. The stairs near the second story landing creaked, and we had to make our way up the side of the stair-case as close to the railing as possible to avoid the noise.

My heart began to race as we drew nearer to the third floor. *This is it! This is what I have been hoping and waiting for since Joan disappeared! She must be close. She has to be!*

I swallowed hard, my eyes wide and dry. I could not afford to miss anything. I listened for Joan, tried my best to hear her voice...but I couldn't. At least not yet.

"Where do we go from here?" I asked Daniel as we reached the third floor.

Daniel looked around. The third floor was much, much smaller than the ground floor, likely nothing more than smaller storage rooms for the main parts of the warehouse below us. The darkness permeated more heavily up here, too, as there were no windows in the main hall.

"We need to take a left up here, and it should be

the first door on the right," he said. "But we must be careful. My nephew may very well be up here, and I have no idea what he might do if we simply waltzed down the hall."

I looked at Miles, and he nodded. "You two wait here. I will make my way over there and see what I can find." He hunkered down, hovering near the wall as he inched his way to the corner.

I held my breath as he approached, and then peered around it. He turned to look at us, and gave us a wave to follow after him.

"No one is there," Miles said, the first sign of a smile spreading across his face. "Let's go try the door."

"I hope we did not come all this way just to be stopped by a blasted door..." I murmured as we started down the hall.

"Never fear, I brought a lockpick," Miles said. "I always have one on me."

I gave him a sideways glance, and he merely grinned at me. It was hardly the time to be disappointed in him, especially if we ended up needing it.

I reached the door first, grabbing hold of the handle – before taking a firm step away. I looked at Miles. "Miles...would you perhaps look inside, and if – if she – "

"Of course," he said, stepping up in front of me. He took hold of the handle, and turned.

The door swung inward, and my heart flipped

inside and out –

"Miles?"

I gasped at the voice, dashing around Miles and throwing myself into the room.

Joan sat in a broken chair along the wall, beside the only grimy window in the whole room that overlooked the city. Slowly, she stood.

I wasted no time. I hurried across the room and grabbed hold of her, pulling her into my arms. I held her as we both cried and laughed, and held on to each other as if we had not seen one another in years. I had never been happier, nor more relieved, than I was in that moment.

"How – how did you find me?" Joan managed to choke out between hiccups.

I pulled away, studying her face. "It's a long story," I said. "Are you hurt? Did he hurt you at all?"

She shook her head, but tears filled her eyes again. "No," she said, rubbing her sleeve over her face.

Miles appeared beside her, offering her a clean handkerchief, which she took, her lower lip quivering.

She wiped her face, clearing her eyes of the tears. "No, he didn't hurt me," she said. "I am fine...except hungry, and terribly, terribly thirsty."

"I imagined she would be," Daniel said, coming into the room, pulling a tin flask from his jacket. He uncapped it and passed it to her. "Go on, take it. It's hot broth."

She eyed him warily.

"He's a friend," I said, knowing it might not be the best time to tell her that he was her kidnapper's uncle.

Joan nodded and took the flask.

"Drink slowly," Miles said. "You might get sick otherwise."

She did so, and her whole face melted with relief. "This might be the most delicious soup I have ever had..." she said, licking her lips, a droplet dribbling down her chin. "Thank you. Very much."

"Yes, thank you for thinking ahead in such a way," I said. "That was incredibly kind."

"It was my pleasure," Daniel said.

"I cannot believe it's really you..." Joan said. She searched my face as if she did not think I was real. "I thought – I really thought that I would be here forever..."

"I wouldn't have let that happen," I said.

"It isn't as if I doubted you," Joan said. "I knew that if anyone could find me, it would be you. I was just..."

"Afraid," I answered for her.

She looked at me. "Yes..." Her eyes narrowed as she gazed at my forehead. "Are you all right? Where did you get that horrendous mark?"

I reached up and gingerly touched the bruise. "It doesn't matter," I said.

"Did you get that just now?"

"No," I said. "Do not worry about me. I'm fine. I am

just worried about you."

"You are safe now, Miss Joan," Miles said, stepping up beside me. "I can assure you of that."

"I know," Joan said. "But how did you know where to find me? How did you find out about Mr. Baldwin?"

"Mother informed me you had been seeing him," I said, crossing my arms. "After some investigating, I learned he had been attending your shows. I assumed that if you and he had been seeing one another, he might be able to help me."

Joan took a long draw on the flask, smacking her lips before frowning at me. "I assume you learned rather quickly that was nothing more than a mistake?"

"Precisely," I said. "He seemed entirely indifferent when Miles and I went to speak with him, which seemed incredibly strange after learning how enamored he appeared to be with you."

"Where did you hear that?" Joan asked.

"Well from someone at the theater, in fact," I said. "The assistant theater director."

"You mean Mr. Willow?" she asked.

"I don't know..." I said. "He is quite tall, thin, and reminded me of a – "

"Lion?" she answered for me.

"Yes, that's precisely it," I said.

She nodded. "He's wonderful. He is the one who put me in contact with the talent scout that I met recently."

"Mr. Beecham?" I asked, tentatively.

She nodded, taking another sip.

"Joan, there is something you should know about Beecham – "

Miles came to my side, dropping his voice. "I understand that you two have a great deal to catch up on, but we really should be going." His face became serious. "We likely do not have a great deal of time."

"It's all right," Joan said, capping the flask again. "They will not be back for some time."

"Why do you say that?" I asked.

Her expression changed from relief to worry again. She brushed some hair from her face. "They are planning to steal a painting. That is why Mr. Baldwin has been trying to romance me for the past month or so."

"A painting?" I asked.

"Which painting, precisely?" Miles asked.

Joan looked between us. "You don't seem surprised. You knew?"

"Some of it," I said, pointing over my shoulder to Daniel who stood near the door. "Mr. Baldwin's uncle informed us."

Joan shook her head in disbelief. "I suppose I should have expected the pair of you to find out all of this."

"Which painting are they after?" I asked.

"The one hanging in the parlor, in fact," Joan said. "The one of the young woman at the washing basin?"

"That Mother always said reminded her of a painting of her grandmother?" I asked.

"It very well might have *been* her grandmother," Joan said. "It was painted by a prestigious artist by the name of Edward Van Huesen almost one hundred years ago."

"Van Huesen?" Miles repeated. "There are several of his paintings in a gallery in London. Rather big name in Europe."

Joan nodded. "Apparently, the painting has been in our family and was brought over with our grandfather when they came from England."

"How did you learn all this?" I asked.

"Well...from Mr. Baldwin and Miss Jacobs," she said.

Miss Jacobs? I thought. *Was that not the young woman Miles and I met at the theater –*

"I overheard a conversation between the two of them just the other day – " Then she shook her head. "No, perhaps I should start with how this whole fiasco began."

"Are you sure we have the time?" Miles asked.

"Yes," Joan said. "They won't be back here until... well, until they've decided to kill me."

I gasped. "What? They said that?"

"Yes," she said. "Once they manage to steal the painting, they'll have no need for me any longer."

Miles frowned, and started off back toward the

door.

"What happened two days ago?" I asked. "One moment, you were in the parlor with me, and then only an hour or so later, you were gone."

Joan nodded. "It...well, it should not have been so worrisome," she said. "I should have known better. I was sitting there in the parlor, waiting for you to come back and sit with me, when there was a knock on the window. It was Mr. Baldwin, and he asked me to come out with him. I...well, I was feeling rather down and had wanted to talk with you about it, but I made a bad judgment on my part and agreed to go with him. I did not suspect what was to happen."

"What did happen?" I asked, eyeing Miles over my shoulder. He seemed to be standing guard. Something told me that he trusted Mr. Baldwin's word about as much as he would have trusted it when we first met him. I wondered if he expected him back. It was best to keep my guard up, too.

"Miss Jacobs joined us, and I returned with the both of them to Miss Jacobs' family home. I left the pair of them alone while I went to use the washroom. When I returned, I overheard them discussing the theft." She wrinkled her nose, sneering. "They mentioned how much of a fool I was, how stupid, and how they could not believe I managed to fall for their ploy. They said the painting of the wash basin girl was as good as theirs. All they needed to do was make sure that I was out of the way before they stole it. They discussed ways to convince me to let them come over and spend the evening, such as dinner with the family or some such. And then..." She practically snarled. "The pair of them kissed, blatantly, right in front of me – I could not stand it. I burst through the door and told them I had heard everything."

My stomach dropped. "And then they took you prisoner, didn't they?"

She reached up and laid her hand across her cheek, wincing. "He...struck me," she said. "And then dragged me off to a closet, where they bound my hands and wrapped a gag around my mouth to keep me from screaming. They kept me there until nightfall, and I assume after Miss Jacobs' family had gone to bed. Then they brought me here."

I shook my head. "So all they needed you for was a way into our house," I said.

She nodded. "In the end, they decided that without my cooperation, they must sneak in and steal it like the petty thieves they are," she sneered. "They were going to try and do it right under our noses..."

"It's all right," I said, wrapping my arms around her again. "You are safe now. They aren't going to harm you, and they are not going to be able to get the painting."

"I don't know about that..." she said. "The painting may already be gone."

13

"Joan, a painting is utterly worthless compared to you," I said.

"I do not think you fully understand," she said, shaking her head. "That painting could be worth millions of dollars."

My eyes widened. "How in the world did they know this when we did not?"

"Ned Baldwin spotted it, the day he walked me home," Joan said. "He came into the parlor and I introduced him to Mother and Father. And it seems that he has a friend who has been trying to collect Van Huesen paintings, trying to locate them as many had come over with families, much like ours, from Europe over the past century."

"And he told you all this?" I asked.

"Gloated, more like," Joan said, frowning. "Said that we were fools for not knowing its worth."

"Well, you and I may not know it, but that does not mean Father doesn't," I said.

"That is something I considered, as well," Joan said. She then turned to Daniel. "And you happen to be Mr. Baldwin's uncle?"

"Yes, Miss," he said, stepping up.

She passed him the flask. "If you were willing to come and help my sister, then I imagine that you do not condone your nephew's actions, and therefore are trustworthy."

"I certainly do not support him," he said. "I am terribly, terribly sorry that this has happened to you. If I had known, I would have done everything in my power to stop him."

"Thank you," Joan said. "And truly, I appreciate you helping my sister."

"I don't know if I would have found you otherwise," I said.

Miles came wandering back. "We really should be going," he said. "I do not like remaining here this long. It's far too dangerous."

"And perhaps we shall intercept the thieves," I said. "If we manage to make it back to the house before they do."

"I doubt we will," Joan said. "They left here before you arrived."

"Well, the best part is that the house is well protected," I said. "They will not be able to get away with it."

Joan frowned.

"Mrs. Riley is there, along with all the kitchen staff," I said. "There is absolutely no chance of them getting away with anything with Mrs. Riley around."

Joan smirked. "I suppose you are right about that," she said.

I glanced back at Miles. "Perhaps you should get a head start, and try to intercept them while I help Joan – "

Miles shook his head. "Absolutely not," he said. "I will not leave your side, either of you."

"But surely – "

"Shh!" Daniel's insistent warning cut through our conversation, and at once, all of us fell silent.

"We should have left half an hour ago," came the hiss of a young woman's voice. "Why are we wasting so much time?"

Joan's eyebrows jumped to her hairline, and she looked at me in horror.

It must be Miss Jacobs! Which means that Mr. Baldwin is here, too.

This was worse than we thought.

"Oh, come off it," came a second voice. Mr. Baldwin's for certain. "I needed to prepare."

"What could you possibly have needed?" Miss Jacobs demanded.

"This," he said. "In case we run into any trouble at the Shipman house. Besides...we will need it again once we get back here for her."

A shiver raced down my spine. He must have a weapon of some sort, and intended to use it against both our family and Joan.

Anger boiled my blood, and I could barely stand the idea of something *else* happening to Joan. I reached out and took her hand in mine.

She squeezed it tightly, her hand shaking ever so slightly.

"We know where the painting is, though, right?" Miss Jacobs asked, her sharp voice clearly heard through the thin walls and door. "Why do we even need her anymore?"

Tapping sounded on the door, and Joan shuddered beside me. "Perhaps we do not," Mr. Baldwin said. "It could be best to get rid of her now. Then we won't have to worry about coming back here at all."

"Right, and what if they follow us?" Miss Jacobs asked. "It could lead them right back here to her!"

"We don't want that," Mr. Baldwin said.

Miles came across to me, and pointed to a stack of broken crates stacked haphazardly in the corner.

I nodded, understanding. I squeezed Joan's hand, and motioned for her to follow after me. Daniel, too.

The four of us crept across the worn floor to the

crates, as quickly as we dared. Miles managed to duck down just as the door flung open.

"So sorry to have to tell you this, Joan, but – Wait just a moment, where is she?" Mr. Baldwin cried.

"What do you mean?" Miss Jacobs asked. "Where else could she possibly be?"

"Not in here," Mr. Baldwin said. He groaned in rage, and stomped out of the room.

"She couldn't have escaped," Miss Jacobs said, hurrying after him. "The door was locked!"

Miles tapped my shoulder, and I glanced at him. He looked past me, over my shoulder, and pointed at the wall.

I turned to see what I thought at first was a shadow. Then I realized it was an actual hole in the wall. Narrow, to be certain, but someone could possibly slip through and out into what I could only assume was the hall. I started toward it, but Miles grabbed hold of my arm. When I turned to look at him, he shook his head.

Then what do you want? I wondered, furrowing my brows.

He leaned closer to me, and whispered directly into my ear. Goosebumps appeared up and down the length of my body. "I shall go and try to create a distraction, so the rest of you can escape."

Daniel, who hovered just behind Miles, leaned forward. "I shall come with you," he murmured to Miles.

Miles nodded, and pressed something cold and hard into my hand. *A knife...*

"You can do this," he mouthed to me.

I swallowed, hoping he was right. I had no choice but to do this.

He clapped Daniel on the shoulder, and the pair of them slipped out through the narrow gap in the wall.

Joan turned to me, her eyes widening.

"Don't worry," I murmured. "I won't let anything happen to you."

I gripped the knife in my hand...and waited.

I did not have to wait long, for shouts echoed from a floor below us. I had no idea how they managed to get down to the next floor, but I could recognize one of the voices as that of Miles.

"What in the – who is that?" Mr. Baldwin cried.

"Wait!" Miss Jacobs called after him.

"Come on, then," I said, pulling Joan out from behind the crates, leading her toward the door. I knew I could not move as quickly as I normally would, and hoped that my aching hip wouldn't give out on me. I gritted my teeth as I squeezed Joan's hand, my injured wrist trembling and throbbing. "Now is our chance."

"Wait, perhaps we shouldn't go through there," Joan said, fear coating her words. "Why can't we go through thc same exit they did?"

I hesitated. It seemed like a gamble either way, didn't it? We could chance going through the door we had entered by, knowing we might follow the same path that Mr. Baldwin and Miss Jacobs had. On the other hand, we could follow Miles and Daniel, and risk running into them all anyway.

"I don't know which is best," I said, cursing my indecisiveness. We were losing valuable time. I pinched my eyes closed, trying to imagine the layout of the building. I was vividly aware of the pain that had been inflicted on my body in the accident, and could barely form clear thoughts.

We had taken the stairs from the end of the hall, around the corner...and would have to creep down several flights before we reached the basement, sneaking past the homeless drunkards, all the while trying to make certain Mr. Baldwin and Miss Jacobs did not hear or see us.

I glanced at the hole in the wall. It obviously led downstairs somehow, as Miles and Daniel had managed to get there quickly, but it might have been on the opposite side of the building, away from the car and straight into danger. Miles had risked his own life trying to cause a distraction so that Joan and I could escape. How foolish would it be to follow him needlessly? And in the shape I was in...I might end up putting Joan in further danger due to being unable to get away as quickly as possible.

I shook my head. We would have to take the risk and try leaving through the door. "Come on," I said, gripping her hand and pulling her with me toward the entrance.

We crossed quickly, spurred on by the very real fear that we could be found out at any moment. We were so incredibly close. We had found Joan, learned the truth, and only had to make it through this last, terrible danger before –

I threw the door open and froze.

Miss Jacobs stood on the other side.

The face I had recalled upon hearing her name had been much prettier than the one that now stood before me. Her thick hair had been pulled into a loose knot at the back of her head, coming loose around her ears. She wore a dark dress with long sleeves and a dark hat on her head to obscure some of her face. When she turned to find us, her large eyes flashed, her face setting in a grimace.

"What are you – Ned! She's escaping!" she shouted. She waited a few heartbeats for a response, then rolled her eyes. "It figures. Fine. I will handle it myself..."

She withdrew a slim pistol from her pocket, and pointed it at the pair of us.

Slowly, Joan and I backed into the room again, both of us raising our hands in front of us. Thankfully, I'd tucked my own knife into the sleeve of my dress. I could only hope that I would be able to withdraw it before I would need it again.

"Where in the world did you think you were going,

hmm?" Miss Jacobs asked, kicking the door shut behind her. "I do not recall ever giving you permission to leave."

Tears splashed down Joan's cheeks, but her face remained resolute. "I thought you were my friend," she murmured.

Miss Jacobs' eyes lit up, and she threw back her head and laughed. "A friend? Really? It is astonishing how gullible you are. Anyone with any sense in their head would have realized that Ned and I were using you. I suppose you artistic types are really all the same, though, aren't you? Daft and dim as the day is long."

I did my best to control my anger. If my head became filled with it, it would cloud any sense of judgment I would have. I could not afford to act rashly, not when Joan and I were at such a disadvantage. What I needed to do now was to find a way out of this mess... and quickly before Miss Jacobs became twitchy.

"So all of it was a lie?" Joan asked, her voice feeble. "All of those walks we took together, the lunches, the stories – "

"You truly believe I would tell you about my real self?" Miss Jacobs asked. She snickered again. "Oh, how naïve. No, everything I told you was entirely invented."

Joan's mouth fell open, but she drew it shut again as her jaw clenched tightly.

"How else could I have expected you to tell me

everything you did about your life?" Miss Jacobs asked. "I learned all that I needed to about your home, about the staff that works for your family, about your family's patterns... You practically gave me a detailed list of what to look for when it came to finding the precise means by which Mr. Baldwin and I could steal that painting."

"Which you have yet to do, I notice," I said, cutting in.

Miss Jacobs' eyes flicked to me with a flash. "How nice to see you again, Miss Shipman. I would like to know how you managed to find Joan, as hidden away as she was."

My eyes narrowed, and I resisted the urge to grab the knife immediately. "I will keep my silence, thank you," I said. No need to give any of my secrets away so freely.

She shrugged. "Not that it matters. I suppose I can kill the both of you."

I grimaced. "And when was the last time that you killed a person, Miss Jacobs?" I asked. "You speak as if it will be as easy as killing an insect."

Miss Jacobs said nothing, but did not lower the gun.

"Why did you agree to this, Anne?" Joan asked. "Did he somehow force you to go along with this scheme?"

"No, I needed no persuading," Miss Jacobs

snapped, her expression darkening. "You do not know the worth of the treasures in your own home. Ned and I will be rich, and we can run away and finally be together without any concern."

"And you trust his word so implicitly?" I asked.

Miss Jacobs hesitated for just a moment. "Y – Yes," she said. "I have every reason to trust him."

"Or he is simply using you..." Joan said. "Without you, he might not have been able to get as much out of me as he did. Now that I know what the two of you were up to, it is clear that you both learned different things from me."

"Do you imagine that the moment you both leave here, and manage to steal the painting, he is willingly going to share all the wealth from it with you?" I asked. "You, who is not tied to him in any meaningful way, bound only by his flimsy word?"

"I'm different from all the other women in his life," Miss Jacobs snapped, her eyes shining.

"Are you quite sure?" Joan asked. "Those were the same words he said to me, when you were not around. The same words he said to a friend of ours, before their relationship ended. He told me that I was different, that he had been looking for someone just like me for as long as he could remember. He told me he had dreamt of me, that he could not get my voice out of his mind – "

"Enough," Miss Jacobs said through gritted teeth.

"You do not have to listen to him," I said, chancing a step forward. "You need not let his lies fill your mind."

"Yes, Anne, please," Joan said. "You will regret this, and for what? For him to end up leaving you behind with nothing more than the guilt of taking the lives of my sister and me?"

Miss Jacobs tossed her hair, an ineffective motion, given that she had no more than a few strands loose around her face. "I don't need to listen to you. Not anymore. I have Ned. He said this was the best way to guarantee that we could be together forever!"

I might have gagged if I was not so terribly frightened. "Miss Jacobs, you are not listening to a word we are saying. We are trying to warn you! Do you really think someone as fickle as Mr. Baldwin would keep his word to you?"

"Has he ever told you that he loved you?" Joan asked.

She blanched, but looked away. "I don't see how that is particularly pertinent," she hissed. "How is it any of *your* business?"

"So he hasn't," I said, shrugging my shoulders. "Then I assume all of these assumptions you have made are nothing more than figments of your own imagination, fed by loose and vague answers on his part?"

"No!" Miss Jacobs exclaimed. "No, he told me that he – that he can't do any of this without me!"

"That much is the truth," Joan said. "He needed you to get to me, taking advantage of your personable character." She shook her head. "Which is a real pity… for you and I might have been real friends if he had never planted these ridiculous ideas in your head."

"We never would have been friends," Miss Jacobs sneered. "You and your kind are too good for people like me. You never would have given me the time of day."

"So you say," Joan said. "You clearly have learned nothing of me during this façade of a friendship."

"Why would I have cared?" Miss Jacobs asked. "All we wanted was that stupid painting."

"You mean Mr. Baldwin wanted it," I said. "Did you even know about it before he told you?"

"No," she said, her eyes flashing. "But is that not the beauty of it? He came to me, told me that he needed my help – "

"What I do not understand is if you met him before or after he asked for your help with stealing the painting," I asked.

I could feel Joan staring at me out of the corner of my eye, likely wondering where I planned to go with this confrontation. If I could talk this woman out of helping Mr. Baldwin, then we would be guaranteed to get out of here alive, but also to have a good witness to hand over to the police to convict Baldwin.

"How long have the pair of you been working together?" I asked.

Miss Jacobs' hold did not ease up on the gun, but she seemed more interested in us than it, for the moment. I wondered if it was even loaded, or simply for show. "We met at a jazz club about a month ago, and got to talking over some drinks. He told me about this wild plan he had, and I told him that I wanted to help. I wanted to split the profits, of course, which he agreed to..."

"But you never anticipated that you would fall in love with him," I said, shaking my head.

"Typical," Joan said, shaking her head, too.

"And now, you are a liability," I said.

"What do you mean by that?" Miss Jacobs hissed.

Joan glanced sidelong at me. "How can he ever be certain you will keep his secret?" she asked. "That you will not betray him one day? A man as clever as him isn't going to leave any loose ends. Certainly, he isn't going to let another person share in his profits."

Miss Jacobs' face fell. "He will have no choice. We have an agreement," she said, but her voice betrayed her unease.

"Of course he has a choice," I said. "When he no longer needs you, he will have no compunction at getting you out of his way...permanently. You have seen already how far he is prepared to go to achieve his aims."

She was silent.

*Perhaps this is the first time we have managed to get through to her...*I mused.

I wondered if I should take a step forward toward her...when there was a sound that sent a cold stab of fear through my insides.

The sound of a gun going off.

I nearly doubled over. Wildly, I looked around at Joan, who busily examined herself, hands sweeping over her stomach and abdomen. She looked up in shock, at me. When we realized that we both were all right, we turned our attention to our surroundings.

...Miles?

My heart thundered in my chest as I tried to calm my thoughts.

This was a bad neighborhood, and it was entirely possible that the gunshot came from another conflict somewhere else. It had been quite close, though... perhaps even just a few floors below us.

Come to think of it, I have not heard a great deal since the men ran off through the hole in the wall...I wondered. Where could they be? What danger might they have gotten themselves into?

Would Mr. Baldwin have killed his own uncle? Would Miles have been clever enough to find a way to get the gun from Mr. Baldwin? I had a great many questions, but could not go seek the answer until I managed to get out from underneath Miss Jacobs' thumb.

Miss Jacobs' breath came in heavy pants across the room. Her hand shook as she held the gun. "Did – did he just kill them?" she murmured. "Then – then I have no choice but to – but to kill you both, then…"

"No," Joan said. "You don't have to do that! You have no idea what that was – "

"Miss Jacobs, listen very carefully to me," I said. "Once you do this, you cannot go back. You cannot change your mind. You cannot do this moment over again. There is no one telling you that you have to kill us. Even if there were, you need not heed such orders – "

"He – he told me that if it came down to it, I would have to kill her," Miss Jacobs said, then shook her head. "N – Now I will have to kill you both!"

Joan looked at me, and I could see the panic in her eyes. One movement, one slight sound, and she would take off running, which would startle Miss Jacobs. That would surely cause her to pull the trigger –

It could not happen. I had to stop it at all costs.

Slowly, I started to bring my hands together, inching them nearer together. My hands were almost touching when Miss Jacobs noticed, swinging her head, and the gun, around to look at me.

"What are you doing?"

"I am sorry, I have this terrible itch on my wrist," I said, scratching furiously at the skin just beneath the cuff of my sleeve. "You see, I have this rash that just – just never seems to go away – "

Her face wrinkled in disgust, but it had been enough of a distraction.

I yanked the thin knife out of its hiding place in my sleeve, the sharp blade slicing through the fabric. I lunged and tossed the weapon as hard as I could in her direction.

I had never thrown a knife before. Apart from handling one at the dinner table, I had yet to use such a thing at all. I knew it was a slim chance that I might succeed, but I needed to do something; I could not have come this far only to lose my life and Joan's. Not after all I had been through in the past forty-eight hours.

The blunt handle of the knife collided with Miss Jacobs' shoulder, causing her to flinch –

A blur of shadow moved beside me, and by the time I had turned my head to follow it, I found Joan wrestling with Miss Jacobs, their hands intertwined around the pistol. They struggled against one another, the end of the gun flailing all around the room –

I leapt out of the way not a moment too soon, before the gun went off with an earsplitting noise.

All three of us shrieked, but only Joan managed to hold on to the weapon as Miss Jacobs threw her hands over her ears and fell to the floor, cradling her head in her arms.

Joan, with a puff of air blowing some of her hair from her eyes, pointed the gun down at Miss Jacobs.

I gaped at her. "Joan...Where did you learn – "

"Don't be too impressed, sister," she said, casting a brief glance in my direction. "I practiced a great deal with Mr. Willow for a play in which I had to perform a similar choreography."

"Well done!" I exclaimed. "Here, let's bind Miss Jacobs' hands."

I picked up the knife from the floor and cut a rough line all the way around my sleeve. As shredded as it already was, it made little sense to try and salvage it. When I had a long, thin strip of fabric, I bound Miss Jacobs' hands behind her back.

"I see you have nothing to say now," Joan said to her.

Miss Jacobs was silent, only scowling at the floor.

"Come on, we have to find the others," I said, pulling our reluctant captive to her feet. "Joan, keep an eye on her while I take the lead."

"Certainly," Joan said. "Come along, Miss Jacobs. Let us go find your lover."

We made our way down the stairs, careful to avoid any encounter with the homeless men. Angry voices bounced up from the depths of the basement, but I did not recognize them.

Where are you, Miles?

We found the front doors, and while we had avoided them upon entering, I knew that a more public entrance would likely be easiest to traverse for the time being. We stepped outside into the bitterly cold night, the lights from the city dancing on the water across the street, partially obscured behind the packing plants.

"There they are!"

My heart pounded at the unexpected voice –

Daniel appeared in a pool of light from one of the few working lampposts along the sidewalk, sweat trickling down the sides of his face. He stopped before us, hands on his knees, panting. "We – we have detained him," he said, pointing down the sidewalk. "Your butler – he is guarding him at the moment. Got the gun away from him."

"Glad to hear it," I said. "Here, you wait with his accomplice. I will go and – "

A wailing of sirens echoed through the night, and a pair of police cars appeared at the end of the street. I had little doubt of their destination, which was assured to me when they pulled up outside the warehouse.

Immediately, I found myself grateful that we had accidentally left the gun upstairs. It would make our innocence more obvious. And with Joan's frazzled appearance and my sliced arm, there would be little doubt as to who the attackers and the victims had been.

"Officers," Daniel said, hurrying to the tall, broad-shouldered man who stepped out of the first car. "Thank goodness you are here."

"We had reports of gunshots," the man said, arching a brow, his gaze sweeping over to where Joan, Miss Jacobs and I stood.

"We were attacked by my nephew," Daniel said. His voice cracked, and I imagined the pain he must be feeling to accuse his own nephew in this way. "He kidnapped that young lady – the one in the yellow."

Joan looked at her dress. It might have passed as yellow, but with two days of dirt and filth caught up in the delicate fabric...

"Around the corner here, you will find my nephew," Daniel said, gesturing down the street. "And here, this woman who has her hands tied is his partner. They kidnapped the young lady and planned to break into her family's home to steal a priceless artifact – "

"All right, sir, calm down," said the shorter officer with a moustache that more than made up for his lack of stature. "We will take witness accounts from all of you."

"One moment, are you the Shipman girl who went missing?" the first officer asked, turning to point between Joan and I.

Joan nodded. "Yes, I am."

"How did you know she was missing?" I asked. "My

father never filed an official report." *At least I did not think he did...*

"A private investigator with connections to our department contacted us yesterday on his behalf, asking us to look around the city in case the father's hunch about her leaving town ended up being incorrect," he said. He smiled at Joan. "Glad to hear that your old man had some sense."

I breathed a sigh of relief. "As am I..."

Joan looked over at me. "Well, that should clear things up, shouldn't it?"

"It certainly should," I said. "We might be in for a long night, though."

"That's all right..." Joan said, grinning at me through the smudges on her face. "I know that at the end of all this, I can go home and have Mrs. Riley draw me a hot, bubbling bath. The thought alone will help me to get through whatever I must."

I grinned at her, as well, and laughed. Soon, she joined me...which drew some rather startled looks from Miss Jacobs and the officers who were leading her away.

14

———

"What am I going to say?" Joan asked as the police car pulled up alongside the sidewalk just outside our home at Sutton Place. She clasped her hands tightly together, peering through the window. "What shall I do?"

"Well, I would prepare to be smothered by Mother," I said.

"Just know that we are all incredibly relieved, Miss Joan," Miles said beside me. "It has been a very long few days. For all of us."

"You are certainly not wrong about that, Miles," Joan said.

The officer turned around in the front seat while his partner exited the car to open the door for us. "Mind if we come in to meet your folks?" he asked.

"Not at all, sir," I said. "And thank you, again, for all your help this evening."

He tipped his hat to us, his moustache stretching across his face like the spread wings of a bird when he smiled. "I'm just relieved that we managed to solve two issues in one evening. When I heard a young lady had gone missing...well, let me tell you that I did not have a great deal of hope. And to think that her sister is the one who found her..." He shook his head. "Isn't that just something?"

"Thank you, sir," I said. "I didn't much care how she was found; I only wanted her to be all right."

"As did we all," he said. "I imagine your folks won't mind too much the hour, even if it is..." He checked his watch. "Half past three, now."

I sighed, exhaustion mingling with the sheer relief of finally, *finally* being at the end of this nightmare.

The taller officer opened the car door for us and helped us out. There were only three of us now, aside from the officers, as we had already dropped Daniel off on our way back from the police station. It seemed Mr. Baldwin's uncle meant to stay with a friend while his nephew's legal issues were sorted out.

We made our way up the steps, and Miles unlocked the front door. The house beyond had fallen asleep; even the clock in the front hall seemed to be resting quietly.

"Shall I go wake them?" I asked.

"No, perhaps I should," Joan said. "Though the surprise of seeing me might stop their hearts."

"They might think you nothing more than a figment of their wild imaginations," I said as Miles closed the door behind all of us.

"Then maybe I should go and wake them," Miles said.

Footsteps sounded on the stairs, and I turned to see Mrs. Riley hurrying down to us, while still tying up her robe. "Who – Oh! My word! Miss Joan, is that you?"

"Yes, it's me!" Joan said.

Mrs. Riley hurried over and threw an arm around her, forgetting all formality. "You – you really are here! But how? Wait, no. Do not tell me." She pulled away and at once turned up the stairs again. "Let me get your parents! Oh, they are going to be thrilled!"

"Should I go with her?" Joan asked.

"Why don't we adjourn to the drawing room?" Miles asked. "I can have a fire set and fetch some tea. The whole family will need time to talk and a comfortable setting for the reunion."

"Very good," I said. "And you should come with us, officers. At the very least to relay the facts to our parents."

We had not yet settled ourselves in the drawing room when Mother and Father appeared.

"Joanie? Is that you? Is it really you?" Mother asked just before she burst into tears. She crossed the room to Joan, and the two held on to one another for a long time, unable to control themselves.

Father strode into the room, and as I watched him, I noticed the tightness around his eyes. He sniffed, and rubbed at one eye before he recovered his composure. He crossed over to Joan and laid a hand on her shoulder.

Joan quickly extracted herself from Mother and threw herself into Father's arms, crying against his chest.

"But how did you find her?" Mother asked. Her eyes fell on the police officers standing near the fireplace that Miles knelt beside, trying to get a fire going. "Oh, officers, how can we ever thank you?"

The policeman with the moustache shook his head. "You are mistaken, Mrs. Shipman. We simply arrived at the scene at the end of it all. Your daughter and your butler are the ones who found her."

Mother turned to look at me, her eyes wide.

"Really, ma'am, it was Miss Sylvia," Miles said from the fireplace hearth, tucking bits of old newspaper between the logs. He struck a match that hissed and flared into a brilliant orange flame. "She is the one who found Miss Joan."

"Sylvie? You found her?" Mother asked.

I looked away. "I did, yes."

I could feel both her and Father's gazes upon me, and found my mind utterly blank.

"Mother...Father..." Joan said. "Sylvia discovered that it was Mr. Baldwin who had taken me."

Mother gasped, clutching at her heart. "Taken you? But I thought you were on your way to California?"

Joan shook her head, looking rather perplexed. "Why would I have gone to California?"

"To visit your aunt," Father said, his brow a hard line. "We thought you were hoping to find your big break out there."

"Heavens, no..." Joan said, frowning. "I gave up that idea long ago. Do you really know me so little?"

Father looked away, and Mother's bottom lip trembled. "Oh, but how were we supposed to know anything was wrong? How could we have known where you had gone?"

"Sylvia told me that you hired a private investigator," Joan said. "Though with her abilities, I am surprised you did not simply ask Sylvia to handle my disappearance."

"Hiring a professional seemed for the best," Mother said.

"There was no reason to put your sister through the agony," Father agreed. "Especially if you were found dead."

Silence passed through the room, and I realized that my parents' concern had been greater than I had realized. All their insistence that Joan would be all right had been to try and ease their fears – and mine.

"Next time, I hope you will listen to Sylvia more," Joan said. "For she was the one who found me."

"Though I will admit that the investigator you hired, Father, passed what he knew on to the police," I said, gesturing over my shoulder to the policemen standing near the fireplace. "They arrived just as we managed to detain Joan's kidnappers."

Mother gasped. "Oh, my!"

Father looked at them, solemn. "Thank you, gentlemen. I truly do appreciate it."

"It was our pleasure," said the taller, broader officer. "We are grateful that this story has a happy ending."

"And they shared with me, Father, that you asked the investigator to spread the word around town..." I said, eyeing him. I did not need to elaborate that it meant he had not entirely believed the California story after all.

He returned my gaze, and gave me a small but noticeable nod.

"My dear, you still have not yet told us exactly what happened?" Mother asked, her hands knit tightly together beneath her chin.

It was Jane's turn to look sheepish. "No, I have not, I suppose. It was...Mr. Baldwin and a woman by the name of Miss Jacobs, both of whom had been trying to befriend me for the past month or so in hopes of using me to gain access to our home. Their plan was to then steal a painting in the parlor."

"Steal a painting?" Mother asked. "Why, whatever for?"

Father heaved a sigh. "Let me guess...the painting of the woman at the wash basin?"

"You knew?" Joan asked.

Father nodded. "I never made mention of it because there are certain people in our family who simply cannot contain themselves when they have exciting news..." he said, giving Mother a sidelong look.

"Joan never would have told anyone," Mother said, looking confused. "Honestly, dear, you really should trust her more – "

"Where have you been all this time, Joan?" Father asked. "You have been missing for almost two days."

"Mr. Baldwin took me to a place downtown, near a fishing cannery," Joan said. "Because I had discovered his plot, he intended to keep me out of the way until he and his female accomplice broke into our house to steal the painting."

"Did anything strange happen tonight?" I asked, looking back at Mother and Father. "Did anyone try to break in?"

Father shook his head, and so I looked at Mrs. Riley who had also joined us.

"No, nothing strange," she said. "I would have certainly noticed if someone was trying to break in."

"They never even made it here, then," I said. "What a relief to hear."

"Oh, Joanie...you must be famished," Mother said.

"I am starting to grow hungry, yes," she said. "Mr. Baldwin's uncle brought me some broth, but that seems to have only awakened my appetite."

"Do not worry," Miles said, getting to his feet. "I have already sent for Gibbons to make something quick for you. He should have something ready shortly."

"But I don't understand," Mother said, shaking her head. "Mr. Baldwin's uncle? Why did he help you?"

"He knew that his nephew was up to something nefarious," I said, answering for Joan.

"Oh, that Mr. Baldwin..." Mother said, brow furrowing. "I knew he was up to no good. Oh, Joanie, why did you not listen to us?"

"Mother, you assume I did not," she said. "I knew that he was a lousy sort, but...he was persistent, and..." She looked disgusted. "...charming, in a strange sort of way."

"You allowed him to lure you into a trap?" Father asked.

"Not precisely, no," I said for her. I could see the hurt on her face. "He came to the house and she went with him and Miss Jacobs to spend some time together.

There she overheard their plans, confronted them, and well...she ended up in a closet until nightfall."

"Oh, dear..." Mother said, reaching for Joan once again. "My poor darling baby..."

Joan allowed Mother to hold her, but gave me a look of apprehension.

"They then took her to the warehouse downtown that once belonged to Baldwin's father before his business went under," I said. "I believe that may very well be where he keeps some other stolen objects."

This caught the attention of the police officers, both of whom looked at me, expressions hardening.

"I noticed while we were hiding behind the crates that two of them were still intact, and had hardly a speck of dust or cobwebs on them. They were rather hidden, but I imagine those are where some other items might be kept. Theft of expensive objects would explain how Mr. Baldwin always had a source of income."

"We will have to go back and investigate," said the broad-shouldered officer.

"He had another accomplice, too," I said. "A friend who collects Van Huesen paintings. That is what they were after."

"I know the name," said the officer with the moustache. "Heard there's been a few of those around the city that have gone missing. I don't suppose you've got a name?"

I glanced at Joan. "Did he ever mention the name of the man who wanted the painting?"

Joan frowned, her gaze distant. "...Matthews, I believe. Oh – wait – no, it was Michaels."

The officer with the impressive moustache pulled a pad out from his coat and jotted the name down. He nodded. "Very good. You have given us some information that we have been looking for since this time last year."

"That's proper detective work," the broad-shouldered officer said to me with a grin. "Well done. Perhaps we ought to consult you sometime with any cases that stump our in-house detectives."

My face flushed, as I tried to decide whether he was being serious or making a joke at my expense. "I – I suppose I would be willing to look at such cases."

"Excellent," said the officer with the moustache.

"Well then, if there isn't anything else, I believe it is time for us to take our leave so that you may all properly celebrate together," said the second officer.

"Thank you for arriving on the scene when you did," I said. "I do not much care to think what might have happened if the kidnappers had managed to break free of their restraints."

Miles saw the officers out while Mrs. Riley went and fetched the meal for Joan.

The housekeeper set a small plate of pastries down before me as well, with a wink. "Miles thought you would be hungry, too," she said before moving on to tend to Mother who had dissolved into tears once again over the whole situation.

"Mother...I feel as if I must apologize," Joan said, spearing a few pieces of potato with the tip of her fork. "This whole fiasco would never have happened if I had simply listened to you and Father from the beginning."

"Oh, Joanie, you do not need to apologize for anything," Mother said. "How could any of us have known that this would happen?"

"But you were right about Ned Baldwin," Joan said, frowning. "And the worst part is that I knew it all along and still allowed myself a chance to get caught up in his attempts to make me fall in love with him."

"It is not entirely your fault," I said. "He managed to make Miss Jacobs trust him, too."

Joan still looked embarrassed.

"Perhaps this will be a good lesson that you can trust your Mother and me..." Father said, sipping his tea. "We do have your best interests at heart, you know."

That made Joan look all the more sheepish.

"I will do my best," she said.

I gave her a gentle nudge with my elbow. "Why don't we send a letter up to Aunt Rachel in Newport? I am sure a change of scene and meeting some new friends might do Joan good after all this. Aunt Rachel is always happy to entertain – "

"Sylvia, do you really think that is wise for your sister, after what she has been through?" Mother asked.

"I do," I said. "She has wanted to take a trip, and this would be a good way for her to get away from all of this for a while."

"Well...at least we would know where she is," Mother said.

"I like the idea," Joan said. "But...perhaps in a few weeks. I think I need to spend some time in the comfort of our own home for a little while before running off on another adventure. I have had enough excitement for some time."

"Speaking of excitement..." Mother said, looking down at me. "You, Sylvia, need to be patched up as well. Where in the world did you get that hideous bruise on your forehead?"

I resisted the urge to touch it. I had no interest in punishing Miles. He did not deserve it, not after all the help he had given me. Father would not think well of him if he learned that he was the one who was driving at the time.

"Part of the investigation..." I said, also hiding my wrist. The bandage had been exposed when the knife sliced through the sleeve of my dress. "I'm fine. I just need a little rest, is all."

Mother seemed relieved, but I knew Joan did not

believe me. I would have to tell her, but not when Mother was around.

It was nearing four-thirty in the morning when Joan was overcome with exhaustion. She fell asleep upright in her seat, and we had to coax her awake to get her upstairs. I told Mother I would help ready her for bed, and asked Mrs. Riley if she would prepare a hot bath for her as soon as she woke. Father and Mother made their ways to bed when they were sure that Joan was settled in and resting.

"She may sleep well into the day tomorrow," I said. "And she will likely be ravenous when she wakes. After a hot bath and a full meal, she will be as good as new."

"I surely hope so," Mother said. "Sylvia...thank you. I do not know if we can ever thank you enough."

"You were right all along," Father admitted. "Without you, I wonder if she would have ever been found."

I did not want to tell him that Miles and I had managed to find her just in time. She would have been at Mr. Baldwin's mercy...and I knew that he had none to give.

"You should rest, too, dear," Mother said. "You look as if you have not slept properly in days."

"I haven't," I said. "Very well. I will head to bed."

I bid them farewell at the stairwell and started down the hall...before stopping just as I laid my hand on my door handle.

Now that the issue with Joan had been resolved, and she was home safe and sound...that left only one more matter that needed to be dealt with.

I turned back and headed down the main staircase. I found Miles starting toward the stairs across the foyer.

He stopped at the bottom of the stairs, even as I paused halfway.

"It seems that you and I are of the same mind," he said, looking up at me. "Were you looking for me?"

I nodded.

He sighed. "I agree that we must resume our conversation, but I think that you need rest, first. I am not attempting to delay, and know that you wish to have this resolved...but I think for now, it would be best for you to wait until you have slept some."

Again, I nodded. "I planned to offer the same solution. Shall we meet tomorrow evening, then?"

"Would eleven be too late for you?" he asked.

"No, that should be late enough for everyone else to be in bed," I said. "And should give us the time we need to talk."

"Good," he said with a nod. "Then I bid you goodnight, Miss Sylvia. And well done, for everything you accomplished today."

"You know that I could not have done it without you, Miles," I said.

He gave a slight smile. "You say that...and yet I

think you are more than capable of these feats without my help."

"So you say..." I said. "Goodnight, Miles."

"Goodnight, Miss Sylvia."

I started down the hall, my mind buzzing with a strange emptiness. Like an attic that had been recently cleaned out, I felt hollow, ancient, and worn.

I washed my face, taking great care to cup some of the cold water to my throbbing forehead. It helped to ease a little of the pain, but I made a note to myself to find some of Mrs. Riley's healing balm for the soreness in my wrist and shoulder the next morning.

It was nearing five o'clock when I finally slipped into bed. The sky outside had turned from black to gray, subtle enough that I could barely make out the shape of the clouds behind the skyline. I could hear cars passing through the streets a few blocks away as the city itself began to wake.

I blinked, my eyes heavy and dry. I could not remember ever feeling this exhausted.

My breathing grew lighter as I lay upon the pillows, and my mind gave way to the bizarre in between world of reality and dreams where the lines blurred and the impossible became possible.

15

All the following day, I enjoyed the company of my family, until at last the hour grew late and everyone retired. Then, the house could almost have been empty, if I had not so recently bid Joan goodnight and watched her wander down the hall, rubbing her eyes and stifling a yawn. The excitement of Joan's return seemed to have sapped Mother of all her energy, and she had fallen asleep in her reading chair well before nine. After Father managed to coax her awake and up the stairs, he must have had little desire to remain downstairs, either. It seemed the sheer relief we all had been feeling was more than enough to drain us. We ate well, laughed well, and slept very, very well.

I would have liked nothing more than to partake in the same rest as the others, but my heart was still uneasy. There was something yet that I needed to take care of.

With a small sigh, I proceeded back down the stairs, picking my way carefully through the dimness. I had no wish to wake anyone by flicking on the hall lights.

The stillness did not frighten me as it had two nights before; Joan's presence assured that. It did, however, fill me with a small sense of foreboding, for I did not know what the night would bring. I had not allowed myself to dwell on the impending conversation as I knew that it would have distracted me far too much from finding Joan, and at the time, that had been more important.

Now...it was time to face this.

I wandered down to the parlor, seeing the flickering light of the fireplace stretching out into the hall. I drew in a deep breath, and paused just outside the reach of the light.

*This can only end one of two ways...*I told myself. *Either he will be innocent...or we will be sending for the police in the morning for his arrest.*

I felt no fear this time when I considered it. I supposed that losing Joan had been a great deal more frightening, and as such, I could face this with less concern. It would be as it would be. I simply needed to face it.

I stepped into the parlor and found Miles lingering

near the fireplace. A rolling cart laden with steaming tea, scones, and my favorite angel food cake sat beside the pair of wingback chairs nearby.

I glanced briefly up at the painting that hung over the mantle, of the young woman at the washing basin. The faint smile she wore seemed to be for me, and it gave me joy to see.

"Good evening, Miss Sylvia," Miles said in a low voice that matched the murmuring of the fire. He turned those bottle green eyes upon me, and I shivered.

Oh, Miles...please tell me that you are the man I hope you are, and not who I fear you may be...

"Good evening," I said.

He stepped in front of the chairs, and gestured to the one nearest him. "I took the liberty of preparing some of your favorite treats," he said. "I realize that after the past few difficult days you have had, you might enjoy something frivolous and simple."

I smiled, despite the reality of the reason we were there. "I appreciate it, thank you."

I took the seat and waited for him to serve me the tea, as well as a slice of the cake. I licked my lips, but lowered the plate into my lap as he swirled some milk into his own tea. "Please, sit down and join me," I said.

He glanced at me over his shoulder, his gaze difficult to read in this light. "Certainly," he said, and did as I asked.

I had rehearsed this several times in the past few hours, and I knew precisely how I wanted to proceed. "Miles, I – "

"Please, Miss Sylvia..." he said, raising a hand. "I do not mean to interrupt you, but I hoped that I might speak first."

I recognized the determination in his gaze. I had already had the chance to say what I had wanted to. I supposed it was time to allow him to give his response. "Very well," I said. "I shall listen."

He nodded, and folded his hands in his lap. "If I remember our conversation correctly, you seemed to be under the assumption that I had...killed my wife."

I did not speak. I held my tongue, and tried my best to let him continue.

"To be perfectly honest, I can understand why you came to that conclusion, given the evidence you found," he said. He sighed, shaking his head. "Perhaps...perhaps it would be best for me to start at the very beginning."

"I am listening," I said, taking a hesitant sip from my tea. *Delicious, just as he always makes it.*

"I will have to go back several years, I'm afraid," he said. "In order for you to understand the full extent of what occurred. I was married, quite happily, in fact. I met my wife through a mutual friend of ours about three years ago now, and we were immediately smitten with one another. We wasted no time, and were married within three months of meeting."

I regarded him with a new eye. *So...he really was married...*I did not understand why I found that so difficult to imagine.

He shook his head, and the shadows aggravated the lines in his face; he suddenly seemed far older than his late twenties. "As you might have guessed, I was not always a butler. In fact, until I met you, I have never held such an occupation. I had plans to acquire my Father's business. He is a prominent horse breeder just outside Gloucestershire, and I spent a great deal of my life in the stables."

My eyes widened. Some of the stories he had told me had been the truth, it seemed. He had been mingling truth with lies, all to protect himself.

He shook his head. "We had...a good life. Everything I could have ever wanted. A lovely home, a stable income. Perhaps the best part was a group of friends that we spent nearly every weekend with, friends I had known since my time in university. I would have trusted each of them with my life. I never had any reason to doubt them."

"Which means that one of them betrayed you?" I chanced a guess.

Miles' face hardened. "It was early summer. I had gone out to the country to visit my father and the stables. He had a rather large purchase and needed help readying the horses. I left my dear Sophia in the care of our household staff and under the watch of some friends who lived nearby, and went on my way late one night. That was Thursday..."

A chill swept through the room, and I realized that what came next must have been what changed his life forever.

"As I was not home when this happened, I have had to piece together the story over time," he said. "Newspaper articles, word of mouth, and from a story that a single friend was willing to tell me before turning me out into the streets."

"Is this what happened in the park that night?" I asked. "If you do not...wish to retell it, I understand."

Miles stared down at his knees. "From what I have learned, a friend of ours took her out one evening after dusk. Sophia often enjoyed late night strolls, as it gave her a chance to look at the stars. It was during this walk that he turned and attacked her, killing her out in the open."

"And the man's name?" I asked.

Miles shook his head. "I have my suspicions, but the point is that whoever it was meant to make her death public and be seen by at least a handful of people...people who would be able to identify him as myself. I imagine he deliberately dressed in one of my coats and hats in order to complete the disguise."

"So this man...he wanted to frame you for her death?" I asked.

"So it seems," Miles said. He shook his head back and forth, frowning. "When I came home, I found the police watching the house. When I went to speak with them, they spotted me at a distance and started to give chase. I managed to lose them as I knew my own neighborhood better than they did. I went to a friend's house to try and lay low, to find some information, but he absolutely refused to see me. He thought me guilty."

"How terrible..." I said. "He wouldn't believe you?"

Miles swallowed hard. "His name is Marcus. He looked me dead in the eye and said that people had seen me, that it was irrefutable...and slammed the door in my face."

I sighed. I supposed I had not been any better, had I?

"I even tried to return home, but as my father had not been at the stables for more than a few hours after I arrived, there was no one to corroborate my alibi. I do not believe he thought me guilty, but he told me to flee and keep away until the whole situation was resolved."

"No one would take you in?" I asked.

"No," Miles said. "And honestly, I believe now that I might have put them in danger if they had."

I tapped my finger against the arm of the chair,

eyeing him. "How did you end up here in New York? If the killer is in London – "

"I managed to convince one of my friends to help me investigate," Miles said. "He agreed to speak with some of my household staff on my behalf about the night my wife was killed. It was...difficult, to say the least, trying to find any information that I could. The killer covered his tracks well, it seemed. What I did manage to learn was that there was a connection to New York, left in a note found inside the jacket he had been wearing when he killed Sophia. He discarded the coat and hat at the park. So...that is how I ended up here."

"Have you been investigating this the entire time?" I asked. "While you have been working for my family?"

He nodded. "Subtly. By letters, mostly. Unfortunately, few people will give me a chance to tell my side of it, as most of London has now heard the tale of the young man who so brutally murdered his wife in the middle of Hyde Park."

"So when I found you that night in the alleyway – "

"It was quite fortunate that you found me when you did," he said. "I had run out of ideas, all my leads had gone dry... I realized that your request would keep me safe and give me the perfect disguise to reside beneath while I searched."

"And your friend – our family friend, who we went

to visit?" I asked. "The Mr. Daniels who repaired my violin?"

"He has been the one friend that I can trust through all of this," Miles said. "He has done a great deal of the legwork for me by finding various newspaper articles and eye witness accounts from the night of the murder. With his help, I have learned a great deal...so much so that I believe I have narrowed down who it might have been."

I shifted in my chair, looking away. "I assume that you had every intention of leaving once you found out what you needed to?"

He sighed through his nostrils. "My intention was to ask for a leave of absence to visit family. I would return to London and hopefully put an end to all of it, clear my name...and then I planned to send a letter to your family explaining precisely what had happened."

"And this person who killed your wife – he has no idea you are here?" I asked.

"If you are asking if you and your family are in danger, I can assure you that you are not," he said. "If it is who I suspect it to be, he would not consider looking for me as a servant anywhere. I do not believe the thought would ever cross his mind."

I breathed easier. "What does all this mean, then?" I asked.

"You believe me, then?" he asked.

I folded my hands in my lap. "I...believe so, yes," I said. "At this point, I have little reason to doubt you."

His eyes widened. "I thought – Well, that is a relief."

"I have worked with you, listened to you, seen your character often enough to know that you can be trusted," I said. "Which is why all of this never seemed to add up in my mind. Something always seemed...off. Your vague descriptions of your life, your unwillingness to discuss your past... That all makes sense now."

He visibly relaxed.

"Besides...there have been too many times where you could have left me to die, especially just last night," I said. "If you were truly a murderer, you could have easily allowed me to be killed along with Joan, and your secret would have died with me."

He nodded. "I suppose my actions will always speak louder than my words, won't they?"

"I suppose they will," I said.

All the tea, the cakes, the treats...all of it lay forgotten on the tray.

"What happens next?" I asked. "Are you planning to return to London anytime soon?"

"I have not learned as much as I had hoped in the past few months," he said. "My plan was to return when I knew for certain who killed my wife...but the trail seems to have grown cold, and I make no further progress from here. Thus, I may not be able to learn anything else without going back myself. Letters can only do so much."

"What can I do to help you?" I asked.

He blinked at me. "You...want to help?" he asked.

"Of course," I said. "Miles, you have put your life at risk to help me resolve several dangerous matters, two of them involving members of my family. It is the least I can do to repay you. Besides, will not two minds working together be better than one?"

"I...suppose," he said. "But your father would never allow you to come to London with me."

"I have an easy solution for that," I said. "I have a friend in England who is to be married very soon, and I should like to be present for it. Father will allow me to go the moment I explain that to him."

He cleared his throat, regarding me with appreciation. "You really would do this for me?"

"Yes," I said. "I would be happy to."

He slapped the palms of his hands against the arms of the chair, a renewed determination on his face. "I can hardly believe it," he said. "After all this time...I am finally going to be able to uncover the truth."

I nodded encouragingly, but secretly, I couldn't help but wonder. Was the truth really what lay ahead of us in London? Or were we about to walk straight into a new danger that was perhaps greater than any we had faced yet?

There was only one way to find out.

Continue the mysterious adventures of Sylvia Shipman in "Murder With Madness: A Sylvia Shipman Murder Mystery Book 6."

ABOUT THE AUTHOR

Blythe Baker is the lead writer behind several popular historical and paranormal mystery series. When Blythe isn't buried under clues, suspects, and motives, she's acting as chauffeur to her children and head groomer to her household of beloved pets. She enjoys walking her dogs, lounging in her backyard hammock, and fiddling with graphic design. She also likes binge-watching mystery shows on TV. To learn more about Blythe, visit her website and sign up for her newsletter at www.blythebaker.com

Made in the USA
Columbia, SC
19 December 2023